Somerset Elm

Somerset Elm

The Journey Begins

JEFF CANFIELD

This is a work of fiction. While some names and events are drawn from America's history, and the story has a historical basis, the words and actions of the characters (other than those which can be verified via historical documents) are the product of the author's imagination, and are thereby fictitious. Other than names and events which are historically verifiable, any resemblance to actual persons, living or dead, events or locales is entirely coincidental.

ISBN: 978-1-58930-207-5
Library of Congress Control Number: 2007907811

For Courtney and Nathan: Tell your generation that the Lord is calling them to serve Him with their whole hearts. And always remember—blessed are the pure in heart, for they will see God.

The Journey Begins

cold wind blew from the north as I made my way across the grounds. One would never guess it was the first day of summer. The biting wind reminded me of the cold and often heartless transition from fall to winter. I was sure of one thing—this was my last stroll across the campus of Yale College. It was only one year earlier, in 1861, that I witnessed the first doctoral degree awarded at Yale. After six long winters and springs in Connecticut, I finally heard the commencement official shout, "Joshua Goodwin Cole, Doctor of Divinity." For me, that was as sweet as hearing the wind gently blowing through the magnificent elms along Somerset Lane near my home in Lawrence, Kansas.

As exciting as it was to be among the first doctoral recipients at Yale, it was much more exciting to take my final stroll across the campus. Homesick does not begin to describe my mood. It bothered me that my family's faces were only memories. When the recollection of your parents and brothers dissolves into nothing more than a dull lithograph in your mind, it's time to go home. It was time for the black-and-white pictures in my mind to take on flesh—the beauty of family replete with hugs and kisses.

A slow run is a more accurate description of how I carried myself back to my dorm room to gather my belongings. After six years of intense studies, I felt as though I could sprint all the way back to Kansas. Soon I would be boarding the train that would return me to the life I left. In a few days I would see my family. The anticipation caused me to burst into my room with excitement.

"What's your destination, Josh?"

I no sooner stepped through the door when my roommate, Harold Richmond, began questioning me. Over the years Harry and I had become as close as brothers. Countless times he nearly drove me out of my mind with his black-and-white view of the Scriptures. Even though I would never admit it to him, I admired his passion. Harry and I had many fervent discussions about the sovereignty of God, predestination, and many other theological topics including the spiritual gifts. Harry had grown up Methodist. He believed in miracles, signs and wonders, and speaking in other tongues. My conservative Presbyterian background caused me to disagree with him much of the time. Despite our disagreements, I had high regard for Harry because he lived what he believed.

Harry volunteered as a chaplain in the Union Army shortly before graduation. To me he looked like the ideal soldier. Stockily built, he stood about five-feet-ten-inches tall. With his dark hair, high cheekbones, and well-groomed beard, he reminded me of many paintings I had seen of valiant soldiers and sailors.

Harry also had an unbending type of intellect that could quickly navigate its way through the most difficult problems. For most of us, panic seems to be the normal and initial human response in the midst of a crisis. Harry, on the other hand, seemed to thrive in the midst of crisis. While working at the New Haven shipyards one summer, I saw an example of his fearless leadership that I will never forget. He and I were unloading cargo on the deck of an enormous clipper, when suddenly several hundred pounds of mast rigging plunged to the deck, crushing one of the ship's seamen. My whole body locked up as I stood in unbelief gawking at the horrible scene. A split second after the loud crash I looked at Harry, and saw his sharp intellect light up behind his keen brown eyes with a fire that shouted, "Get out of my way!" Immediately he began pulling wood and canvas off the poor soul while giving orders to sailors whom he didn't even know.

Concerning the war, being a staunch abolitionist Harry couldn't wait to jump in the fray. Heaven help the enemy if the Union Army ever put a weapon into his hands. He would think nothing of leading a charge directly into an entire regiment of Confederates—believing at every moment the victory belonged to him.

Needless to say, Harry kept up on the progress of the war, and because I was his roommate, he also kept me abreast of new developments. Before volunteering, Harry told me that the Union Army called for 500,000 new soldiers and, according to the government, each regiment was required to have a chaplain leading to a tremendous need. Even though Harry was not given an official rank, chaplains customarily were treated as captains.

He would not begin serving until after graduation. Nevertheless, after he told me of his enlistment, I would rush ahead of him and hold the door as we entered the campus dining hall, salute him, and say, "After you, my captain," receiving a playful shove in return. Unfortunately for me, I never learned my lesson. Not knowing his own strength, a playful shove from Harry usually hurt.

"I'm going home," I answered his question.

"You know what I mean, Josh. What does God have in store for you? Have you asked the Lord what His will is for your future?"

"Yes, Harry. I believe He is telling me to go back home and take a church."

I felt extremely guilty for lying to my best friend. But I knew Harry would never leave me alone unless I assured him that I had prayed about my decision to return to Kansas. I had not asked the Lord specifically what He desired for me to do. Unlike Harry, I did not believe that God orders every little step we take. I felt good about going home, so why should I bother the Lord?

Harry and I agreed that God has granted mankind free will in regard to spirituality, and in making moral and ethical decisions. However, I was of the opinion that somehow this free will must be enveloped in God's predestined plan for our lives. We also agreed on Romans 8:28—that all things work together for the good of those who love the Lord. This led me to the conclusion that whatever I decided to do, God would see to it that it was part of His plan. I was convinced He had all my steps ordered. My obligation to His plan was simply to live, breathe, and believe. After all, God is sovereign. His plans will come to pass regardless of whether I fast and pray as Harry does concerning decisions he makes.

In my opinion, Harry's theology was very self-centered. By constantly petitioning the Lord, I viewed Harry's prayer life as saying, "Yea, oh Lord, pay attention to me!" Later I would realize it wasn't Harry's belief that was self-seeking—it was mine. Not only was Harry determined to *seek* God's will, but also to *do* God's will. I did whatever I desired and trusted that God would work it all out for my benefit. Many of my thoughts and beliefs about God, however, were about to be challenged in ways I never could have imagined. I was about to take a journey in my life—a journey which would teach me that having a doctorate in theology did not supply me with all the answers. Looking back, I thank God that He provided for me, even in my ignorance.

We had been through a lot together; so much that a handshake was not sufficient as Harry and I said good-bye—possibly for the last time. As we hugged each other, we knew that our friendship would always be strong within. Memories are God's gift to those who must travel separate paths. Yet, as I left the dorm that afternoon, I thought it strange that two men can become as close as brothers and then leave, knowing that the years spent fussing, fighting, laughing, working, and breaking bread together might be consigned only to a memory. I rehearsed those memories in my mind while waiting for the train. I was afraid if I didn't, I would lose them forever.

Excitement filled my heart as I boarded the crowded train to leave Connecticut. The line moved slowly into the passenger cars to the left and to the right. When it was my turn, I took a step up and then waited. The air smelled of oil, carpetbag, worn-out leather, and hand-rubbed steel. For the most part, the other passengers were patient and quiet. After walking through two passenger cars containing rows of old red leather seats with very little padding underneath, I found one vacant. I didn't look forward to sitting for long periods of time. How-ever, I did feel fortunate to find an open seat.

I was pleasantly surprised to see a young woman sit-ting across from the empty seat. Desiring to be a gentleman, I asked her if the seat was taken. "No, please sit down," she replied. I thought I sensed some angst in her voice, yet, the smile on her face implied she was glad I wore a suit and not a uniform. I was in such a hurry to get settled in for the long trip that I didn't take a good look at her until the train started to jerk and pant its way to full throttle.

At first I looked up and down and across the train car—in every direction except hers. My mind began to paint the picture of her hair, her smile, her eyes, and her facial features on the canvas of my memory. Suddenly, I realized I was sitting across from one of the most beauti-ful young women I had ever seen. Her blonde hair rippled like soft golden waves in the cool breeze coming through the open windows. Her smile was so genuine that I felt I would surely offend her if I did not strike up a conversa-tion. She wore a royal blue dress that displayed a modesty I feared was lost in a nation thirsty for blood. As captivating as all these features were, it was her blue eyes that caused me to feel frozen in time. Thank goodness, the conductor freed me from my gaze.

"Tickets please…Lawrence, Kansas. You have a long trip ahead of you, young man. Be sure you switch trains at St. Louis."

"Thank you, sir," I replied, jolted back into reality.

My mind came back to the turbulent times of the early 1860s. The nation was torn by war. In 1860, slavery was outlawed in Kansas. The following year, the territory officially became a state. Even prior to that time, Kansas was known as a safe haven for runaway slaves. I was returning to a land that was heavily populated with abolitionists and, as a result was a favorite target for Confederate guerrillas. Both my father and grandfather were deeply involved in the Underground Railroad. If the South developed any type of stronghold in Kansas (Lawrence being near the Missouri border), my family would be in grave danger.

Though many on the train were anxious over the present crisis, they tried not to show it. They smiled when I looked at them, but then quickly turned and stared out the window or returned to their newspapers. Their smiles weren't normal or happy. It was as if they were saying, "I'm only smiling to be polite, but inside I'm nervous and worried about the future." The fact that the train was full of Union Army enlistees, lots of blue uniforms, and rifles didn't help. Everywhere I looked, I was reminded of the war. While waiting to board the train I overheard that many of the soldiers were headed to Camp Butler in Illinois for training. They wore the same solemn faces as many of the passengers. I couldn't help but think that if I were in their boots, I would feel like a sheep heading to the slaughter.

One hour into the trip I couldn't stand it any longer. I had to strike up a conversation with the beautiful young woman with whom I kept trying to avoid eye contact.

"My name is Joshua Cole. Forgive me for being so forward, but we do have a long trip ahead of us. May I ask your name?"

"My name is Elisabeth Morgan, and thank you for asking. I was thinking the same thing, but I didn't want to seem forward either. I overheard the conductor when he mentioned Lawrence, Kansas. I'm on my way to Topeka."

"What a coincidence! It looks like we'll have ample opportunity to visit. Have you enjoyed being out East?"

"Yes, I've enjoyed my trip immensely! Have you been out here long?"

"I just graduated from Yale College," I said proudly—too proudly. "I'm going back home to take a church. The minister in the church my family belongs to joined the Union Army, and they've asked me to take his charge."

"Oh, how wonderful! My father is a minister in Topeka. I'll be sure and tell him about you."

"What church does your father pastor Elisabeth?"

"He pastors the largest Free Methodist Church in Topeka. We've just experienced a marvelous revival! God has done some miraculous things! Now I know why the Lord delayed my trip back home. If I traveled yesterday, I would have never met you."

At that very moment a thought soared through my mind and, looking back, I'm sure I must have had a blank look on my face. I was convinced Harry had petitioned the Lord to send this woman in order that she might sit directly across from me and tell me about miracles, signs, and wonders all the way back to Kansas. This notion may have been incorrect, but my assumption concerning the conversation's subject matter was right on target. I was subjected to one miraculous story after another all the way to Indiana!

I had several opportunities to find another seat, however, I kept thinking, "Our next conversation will surely be different" but in vain. They were all the same. I had never encountered a woman who enjoyed quoting Scripture as much as Elisabeth. By the time we arrived in Indianapolis, my brain felt like it had worked an entire week unloading ships in New Haven.

As we pulled into the Indianapolis station, I stood up and stretched—for the first time since we left Ohio. The small amount of padding had conformed so well to my lower parts that I was sitting directly on the hard metal bench. My backside was in pain. I stood up just as the train steward entered our car and informed us that we would have a three-hour delay. As rude as it sounds, I hoped I could covertly separate myself from Elisabeth and find a different seat when I returned to the train.

Elisabeth was attractive, polite, and pleasant company. She was a breath of fresh air compared to the women I had met in Connecticut. It would be an enormous understatement to say that those I encountered around the New Haven docks lacked virtue. A local minister told me that many of those soiled dowds grew up with fathers who, when they weren't drunk, were out to sea for a year at a time. Sadly, these desperate young women searched in every dark corner for love and affection, only to be taken advantage of by those who were less than men, and behaved no better than dogs. Then there was the other end of the spectrum: well-to-do women who invited themselves to every social gathering on campus in hopes of finding their future husbands. Interestingly, after spending considerable time amongst the upper-class, I discovered the same lack of virtue in these women as I found at the docks. The only difference was, their immorality was hidden behind fancy clothes and refined speech.

Part of me desired to get to know Elisabeth better. Yet, there was something about her that bothered me. After visiting on and off through Pennsylvania and Ohio, I finally put my finger on what it was—something that, because of my pride, I would never admit to a soul. I was intimidated by her knowledge of the Bible and her passion for God. Scripture rolled from her lips as quickly as the trees passed by the windows of the train. Elisabeth had obviously been taught well, and she was not afraid to express her beliefs. That part of her personality reminded me of the element I enjoyed of Harry's personality. But he was a man. I felt comfortable arguing, and sometimes even yelling, at him. It never upset him. He would simply shake his head and roll his eyes. It also never affected our friendship. If anything, our passionate discussions drew us closer.

As chauvinistic as it may sound, I could not have those types of discussions with a woman. Many times within our discussions I desired to give Elisabeth a stern retort but held my tongue. I discovered that it wore me out mentally to allow my mind to race and formulate without sounding a response. I had to hold it all inside so I could keep up the gentlemanly standard with which I had been raised. In that sense, I wondered if she was knowingly taking advantage of me. Even if she wasn't, that was how I felt. As beautiful as she was, I considered this part of her personality to be very impertinent which, in turn, rendered her unattractive. Nevertheless, I felt that I would be a fool to shut the door where the potential for a friendship was concerned. For now, I just needed a rest.

When the conductor yelled, "All aboard," I made my way toward the front of the train. I couldn't help but notice a sifting of the passengers. This time the soldiers grouped together and moved toward the cars in the rear, while those in civilian attire moved toward the front cars. I also noticed that our train no longer had a storage car between the coal car and first passenger car to serve as a buffer. Just the same, I boarded the front passenger car— the last choice of most of the travelers as it was the noisiest and filthiest. At the station I learned that the military— transporting a shipment of munitions—had requested the storage car be moved toward the rear of the train for fear of sparks from the engine. That would explain our three-hour delay.

After boarding the train, I sat down across from an older gentleman and his wife. They smiled at me, and then withdrew into their privacy. She would whisper to her husband while looking at him over her reading glasses, and then stick her nose back into her book. The husband would whisper a response and then look out the window.

Sitting next to me was a plump middle-aged man whose body language made it plain that he desired to be left alone. I could tell he wasn't asleep, yet he had his arms crossed, eyes closed, and wore a scowl on his face. This was all well and good. Finally, peace and quiet…well, as quiet as it could be so close to the engine. Aided by the rhythmic chug, I managed to fall asleep with my head in my hands. Suddenly I felt a gentle tap on my shoulder.

"I kept turning around and looking at you from behind, but I wasn't sure if it was you."

There was Elisabeth, sitting right behind me! The seats of this particular car were arranged so that passengers were in groups of four. We were both sitting on the aisle, and Elisabeth's seat was back-to-back with mine. She must have boarded after me because I certainly would have noticed her sitting so close. I had my head down before the train left the station, so she probably didn't recognize me when she sat down.

"Joshua, I've been thinking about what you said earlier concerning whether or not the Lord actually cares about every step we take." She picked up our conversation right where we left off in Indianapolis. "While we were waiting at the station I looked up several scriptures. Psalm 37:23 says, 'The steps of a good man are ordered by the Lord: and He delighteth in his way.' And then, Proverbs 20:24 says, 'A man's goings are of the Lord; how can a man then understand his own way?' That's why we have to pray and trust that God is directing all of our steps. He orders our paths."

"Elisabeth! May we stop discussing doctrine, please?"

"I'm sorry, Joshua. I guess I just assumed you must enjoy discussing the Bible."

"I'm sorry I sound cross, Elisabeth. I've been absorbed in biblical studies for six years and feel as if there's a whirlwind in my head. I need a sabbatical. I apologize for being so rude, but I'm very tired and I would just like to rest for a while."

"I'm sorry," she apologized. "I'll leave you alone."

I felt terrible for treating her that way. She had done nothing wrong. However, I was being honest when I said I needed a rest. The gentleman sitting next to me was large enough that every time the train bounced, his bounce caused an equal reaction on my end of the bench. It was like getting a double-bounce. Even though my mid-sized 180-pound frame couldn't compete with my rotund neighbor, somehow I managed to sleep most of the way to St. Louis.

"St. Louis! St. Louis!" The conductor's call awakened me. I needed to switch trains.

After asking the conductor where to board the train for Kansas City, I hustled to retrieve my trunk and suitcase from the porter, then walked along the deck looking for my train. St. Louis had a fabulous station with nearly thirty tracks side-by-side. I had been sleeping so soundly, and awakened so suddenly, that it took several minutes for my eyes to focus and for my body to feel alive. After spotting the correct train I hurried toward a man in a conductor uniform.

"Is this the train to Kansas City?"

"Yes sir, deposit your luggage and board anywhere you like." The conductor pointed to the baggage cart.

I stepped up into a passenger car four cars from the engine. As I looked for a seat, I noticed that there were no soldiers on this train. Then I remembered they disembarked somewhere in Illinois. I must have been completely worn out to sleep so soundly that I missed a company of soldiers getting off.

The train whistled several times and began to pull out of the station. I was now headed northwest through Missouri toward the border of Kansas. Unlike my earlier experience, this car was quiet. Many of the windows were open slightly—creating a nice gentle breeze. I was so thankful to begin the last leg of my trip home after two continuous days of travel.

Halfway through Missouri, it dawned on me that I had not seen Elisabeth when I switched trains. Suddenly I felt sad. This would have been an ideal time for a lengthy discussion. More than likely I had offended her as we were leaving Indianapolis, allowing my weariness to give way to rudeness. She was probably glad to get away from me.

I had many hours to contemplate our intense discussion from Connecticut to Indiana. I wish we had spent more time getting to know one another, rather than discussing theology. Even though much of the time I was irritated with her bold Christian manner, overall one might have considered our first acquaintance somewhat pleasant if I had not ended it so abruptly. I made a decision that after I got settled in at home, I would make the short trip to Topeka and apologize to Elisabeth in person. As we made our way through the hills of Missouri, I began to daydream about what that day might be like.

Home again – Facing the Danger

"Connelly Junction!" the conductor hollered.

This time when the conductor yelled, I wasn't asleep. I was almost home. Connelly Junction consisted of a watering station and telegraph office for the railroad just one mile south of Kansas City. This is where my family would meet me with the wagon, and we would travel the final portion of the trip together.

As I got off the train I saw my father waving in the distance. I could spot him easily in any crowd. At six-feet-three-inches he was nearly as tall as President Lincoln. Father wasn't obese, but he was a big man with the strength of an ox. Even at a distance I could see him smiling from ear to ear, and waving both of his big hands as he yelled, "Joshua! Joshua!" I dropped my trunk and case and ran to meet him. I was only a couple inches shorter, but due to his broad shoulders, when he hugged me I nearly disappeared in his arms.

After a long embrace, and several pats on the back, Father said, "I sure have missed you son!"

"I couldn't wait to see you either, Pop! Where's Mother? And where's Raymond and Jordan?"

"They're at home with your grandfather, and they're all anxious to see you."

I was sure that Mother would be safe with my grandfather, and my brothers Raymond and Jordan at home. But as dangerous as the countryside could be, I was a little surprised that Father had come alone. As I climbed up in the wagon I noticed the pistol beside him, and a rifle in a sheath strapped underneath the bench. Father was a peaceful God-fearing man, but he was not afraid to use a gun if necessary. I felt safe alongside of him as I loaded my trunk and suitcase and settled into the wagon.

"I wanted to come by myself, Joshua. That way you and I could spend some time together on the way back. I'm sure you noticed that I brought the camp irons. I thought we would spend the night under the stars. It will be like old times."

The "old times" Father was referring to was the nearly six-month-long operation of transporting people and supplies to Kansas. Part of our pioneering expedition was done by rail and the other by wagon. Our family was among the first group of people from the New England Emigrant Aid Society to settle in the territory. My parents, and especially my grandparents, had been good friends with Amos Lawrence, the founder of the society. Amos was a devout abolitionist. He owned many large textile companies in the East, and supplied the means for the original settlers of our town to travel to Kansas. He was also responsible for many buildings, businesses, and private homes being built.

Even though Amos was advancing in years, he continued to supply finances every year for more abolitionists to settle in the town the grateful people had named after him. That's also how the town of Lawrence became known as an abolitionist's town—a garrison for runaway slaves—and why the Confederates hated Lawrence and its citizens.

As we left Connelly Junction, I began to think about our move to the Midwest. It was difficult, but exciting. I was only fifteen years old when we began our journey west. However, because of the responsibilities of traveling and helping to oversee a long journey with a young family, my father and grandfather treated me like a man. During our journey I helped load and unload train cars, and also took turns at the reins of one of the wagons. I hunted with them, fished with them, and even stood watch at night with a rifle. When traveling with the wagons, it was my job each night to set up the "camp irons"—the iron skillets, iron fire grate, and the iron pots and hooks. As I reflected, I understood how being trusted with meaningful responsibilities as a teenager gave me confidence later when I struck out on my own.

As we rolled across the border into Kansas, I told Father stories about Harry, and how he challenged our professors with questions about miracles, prophecy, and speaking in other tongues. Father just shook his head and laughed when I told him how red faced one professor became as Harry chased him in theological circles concerning election and predestination.

"Son, there's just some subjects that we have to agree to disagree with other Christians about, and then love them with God's love even though we don't see eye to eye. It's important in life to choose the battles that matter the most, and understand that the love of God is more important than winning every battle—it's His love that wins the war."

"I agree, Pop, but with Harry every battle was equally important. And you know, as adamant and overly passionate as he was, I always saw the love of God in his life. He just displayed it in a different way. He's the kind of man who will argue with you one moment, and be willing to die for you the next."

"I'd like to meet him someday, Joshua. He sounds like a fine man." Then, changing the subject, "Tell me about your train ride. I'll bet it was long and boring."

As soon as Father mentioned my train ride, there was a pause, followed by a big smile on my face, that he couldn't help noticing. It was the kind of smile that another man immediately understood—especially a father. A smile sparked by a wonderful memory.

Father grinned as he asked, "Who is she? Where's she from? Don't keep any secrets from me, son."

The smile on my face began to vanish as I explained, "The truth is, Pop, I may never see her again. Or if I do, it might not turn out very well. Her name is Elisabeth Morgan and she lives in Topeka. Her father is a Free Methodist pastor. Pop, she's beautiful—probably the most beautiful and wholesome woman I've ever met."

"So what's the problem, son?"

"I'm pretty sure I offended her."

I told my father what happened on the train, and how rudely I treated Elisabeth. After I finished telling him the story, he looked at me with disappointed eyes and shook his head. Then he began one of his lectures, which I certainly deserved.

"Joshua, whether or not you ever develop a friendship with this young woman, at the very least you owe her an apology. You're better than that, son! We raised you to be a gentleman. Furthermore, I cannot believe that you would be the least bit irritated by a virtuous young woman because she loved talking about the Bible! What got into you, son?" Father gave me a playful punch in the shoulder that nearly knocked me off the wagon.

After Father finished his lecture, two things began to sink in my thick skull. I realized that I really must have been out of my mind to behave so rudely toward Elisabeth. I treated her as I would have treated Harry— say whatever I desired and then expect everything to be fine between us. What was I thinking? I had been completely selfish and, as a result I may have missed my only opportunity to get to know her better. The other thing I realized was how soft I had become during my last year at Yale. Father's playful punches never used to hurt. I couldn't wait to get back home and chop some wood. I needed to toughen up.

As the night settled in, we found a perfect spot along a creek to set up camp. The feel of the camp irons brought back many wonderful memories. Sitting beside the campfire, with beans and ham cooking in the skillet on the fire grate, and the smell of the woods and the beauty of the night sky—I felt fifteen again. After supper I sat quietly, mesmerized by the shimmer of the fire, which in a split second lit up bits and pieces of the forest before being consumed again by the darkness.

As I enjoyed the moment I considered how the Lord had blessed my life. There was richness in our family that had nothing to do with wealth. There was security in our family that had nothing to do with power. The security was in the love that we had for each other no matter how difficult the days became. At that moment I knew I would rather be eating supper under the stars with my father than to be anyplace else on earth.

"Joshua, we need to talk." My father interrupted my reverie.

"What's bothering you, Pop?"

"Son, we've had several threats on our lives back home—not only us, but a lot of families in town. There have been notices nailed to the doors of businesses, one threatened to kill women and children. Another one stated that the Confederates were going to burn the newspaper down. Truthfully, son, the entire town is in danger."

Our family owned and operated the *Herald of Freedom*—one of the many abolitionist newspapers the Confederates loved to hate. We began producing the paper shortly after settling in Kansas. The logistics of getting supplies, and the effort it took to train employees, stretched our family's time and patience to the limit. Nonetheless, the newspaper was extremely important to my grandfather and Amos Lawrence. They understood the impact the printed word had on the attitude and resilience of the settlers.

Whenever the local militia would return from an encounter with Confederate guerillas, those in charge would share the events first with the Herald of Freedom, and then we would report the victories to the community. This of course enraged Confederate bandits. Thus, our newspaper not only served the purpose of promoting the abolitionist's cause, but on a more practical level it kept the community notified of everything from free lumber to the settling of grievances.

The most difficult chore for our newspaper was the death notices. In the early days of the settlement, many folks battled typhoid and cholera, and there were several brief periods when we ran death notices every week. The reprint of major news items concerning the war, or reprints of thought-provoking articles, were also vital to our community.

After being safely tucked away at Yale, I had to get used to the idea of being on the frontlines of conflict. As Father told me of the threats, I realized I had not only become soft physically, but emotionally. I had to quickly come to terms with the fact that our family was a primary target. When I left for college, abolitionism was mainly a political issue. Now, with a civil war raging, it was a cause people were giving their lives for on a daily basis. I'm sure Father could sense the fear in my voice as I asked, "Is it safe to go back? Maybe we should get Mother, Raymond, and Jordan and get out of town."

"That's what I want to speak to you about, son. There's comes a time when you have to decide what you believe, how much you believe it, and then stand by it with every muscle in your body. Your mother, brothers, and I feel very strongly that slavery is an abomination in God's eyes. Don't misunderstand—a godly man should always walk away from a meaningless fight. Don't ever break a knuckle on a foolish man. But son, there are some fights that a righteous man must fight. There are righteous causes that are even worth dying for. God loves the souls of the slaves as much as he loves ours. That means our Savior died for them, and they should be as free we are.

"This fight is not going away," he continued fiercely, "and son, I'm not going to turn and run from it. There is no corner of earth that a cowardly man can run to that will make his problems disappear. The disease of cowardice will always be with him. Before Reverend Wilson left to join the Union Army, I remember him saying, 'If a Christian does not give aid to a helpless man, then he has not followed the call of Christ.' Joshua, we decided a long time ago that we're going to face the problem, and fight back."

I listened to my father intently. I knew he wasn't calling me a coward. If he were, he would have come right out and said it. In his own way he was letting me know that he wasn't sure how I would react if I came face-to-face with the decision to kill or be killed. He was reaffirming the fact that our family was not going to run away in the face of danger, and it was time for me to get it settled in my heart.

The following afternoon as we came to the ferryboat crossing at the Kansas River, I was still mulling over the discussion that Father and I had. Lawrence was just on the other side of the river. Inside, part of me was yelling, "Run away!" But my father's words gave me courage. I knew he was right.

∽

As we entered the city, I was astonished at the growth. So much had changed in the six years I was away. When we settled in Kansas, the town had only a couple hundred people. Father told me Lawrence now had over two thousand residents. As our wagon rolled through town, I could see many fine looking houses. Only a few of the original cabins remained, and they were being used as trading posts or specialty stores. Lawrence had become too sophisticated for pioneer cabins—now they were only novelties. Along with two hotels, there were also many other stores and businesses, and even an armory and a jail. Lawrence was no longer just a settlement—now it was a city. In just eight years the town had grown from infancy to adulthood.

Our house on the north side of town was among the finest in Lawrence. Amos Lawrence himself had sent an architect, laborers, and plenty of money to build it. Without a doubt he was a generous man. Although he had an ulterior motive when he financed the building of our house, it was an amiable partnership due to the fact that our family agreed with his vision of Kansas entering the Union as a free state. As planned, our home became a well-known refuge, a spectacular house for receiving, hiding, and redeploying runaway slaves. Unfortunately, I only had the opportunity to enjoy our home one year before I left for Yale. When I departed for the East, I took with me fond memories of helping my father and grandfather build the house, and for a short time being able to lend a hand to the Underground Railroad.

I remember my family receiving runaway slaves—or "passengers" as they were called—in the middle of the night. This was an obvious tactic, but still the most practical. There were three outside entryways into our cellar. Two of them were well hidden behind bushes, and difficult to detect unless a person closely searched for them during the daytime. The third was a normal-looking cellar entrance. It was functional, and necessary to keep up appearances, but it would not lead anyone to runaways in the cellar. We accessed the runaway portion of the cellar through a trap door in the pantry. Father and Grandfather built a large pantry shelf with thick oak casters on the bottom. These casters were barely visible unless a person put their face down on the floor. Amazingly, even when the pantry was full of canned foods and preserves, it would roll smoothly out of the way in order to expose the trap door.

There were thick woods about thirty yards from the rear of the house. At nighttime, during the construction of the cellar, we dug a tunnel from the cellar to the tree line. The Kansas River was on the other side of the woods. Our link in the Underground Railroad had become very proficient at transporting the passengers in and out of town, and then northwest on the bank of the Kansas River to the Big Blue River. If there were no reports of imminent threats, two of us led the runaways into the woods and directed them to their next connection. When they had to leave in a hurry, we worked with them the best we could to explain how to navigate the woods to the next stop. I recall several occasions when we jumped to the cellar floor shouting, "Go! Go! Go!" as we uncovered the door to the tunnel and gave our passengers a hurried departure into the darkness. It gave me a pit in my stomach when I watched them dissolve into the dark tunnel, and then sealed it up, not knowing what their fate would be.

The vast majority of the townspeople were active abolitionists. With our home being the focal point, and the last stop before sending runaways to the next link, community members kept our family well supplied with food and clothing to give our passengers. Though we always had plenty of food in our house, those on the railroad to freedom ate first. I remember once when my youngest brother Jordan took a piece of ham before we had served the runaways in the cellar. Without any hesitation, Father grabbed his hand and swatted him on the rear end, saying sternly, "Jordan, you're free! You can eat anytime you want—don't ever forget that!" Jordan never did forget that moment. Father instilled in all of us a passion to care for those who were less fortunate than ourselves.

Most of the runaway families were broken—mothers clinging to only one of their children while still grieving over leaving their husband and other children behind. Very seldom did we ever see an entire family intact. Many of the adults, and even some of the children, had scars on their faces and backs from being whipped and beaten regularly. Assuming we would have very little time, our family sprung into action the moment we knew passengers would be arriving. We laid out clean clothes, food, and filled two washtubs with hot water. Mother cared for the women and children first, gently guiding them through the process while the men took care of the male runaways. We could bathe, clothe, and feed five passengers in thirty minutes. Afterward, we burned their old clothes that were usually tattered and reeked of sweat and river mud.

We housed our passengers in the cellar until we got word that the next link was stable and secure. Still, we had very little time to get to know folks as they came through. Most of the adults were very untrusting of white folks; also many could not speak or communicate well. My brothers and I would spend as much time as we could afford trying to teach them words and phrases. Often it seemed rather futile, given the small amount of time we had. As I recall, however, it provided a diversion and seemed to bring a sense of calm into their lives. Yet, I will never forget the look of hopelessness in their eyes. It's as if they knew down deep inside that even if they made it to the far north, they would always be runaway slaves. Without a doubt, hopelessness is one of the worst of all human maladies.

The part of our property that I loved the most was the lane that led up to our house. It was approximately one hundred and fifty yards long with fabulous elm trees on either side. We often wondered if the trees had been purposefully planted, or whether former pioneers had cut down the trees in between and around them to create a wagon trail. At the time we settled, wagon ruts were already pressed into the ground between the trees.

We placed a bench on either side of the lane at the end where the house stood. On a regular basis I would sit watch on those benches while reading a book (usually the Bible) with a tin cup lying beside me on the bench. Whenever someone I didn't recognize came into the lane, I tapped the tin cup on the side of the bench. There was no need to tap loudly as every member of our family had their ears attuned to recognize the tapping, and those inside the house would scurry to make sure everything that needed to be hidden was securely tucked away. Those on the outside made sure nothing looked suspicious, and acted as normal as possible. Father or Grandfather would always be the first to greet a stranger. With Confederate guerillas constantly afoot, and many times looking and acting like regular townspeople, we did not trust anyone we did not know. Somerset Lane played an important role in our work as abolitionists.

Once, a friend of ours back East asked Father why he named our lane Somerset. Father explained that when we homesteaded the land and he staked out the property, he found a small crudely fashioned cross near the woods that had fallen over from neglect. The settlement of Lawrence was located between the Oregon and Santa Fe Trails of the early 1820s, and Father surmised that an early pioneer had traveled through and probably lost and buried a loved one. The rough carving in the cross simply read "Somerset."

Father was a very compassionate person and he could not bear the thought of tossing away the cross as if it were nothing more than some old kindling, especially if it embodied the memory of someone's loved one who was laid to rest on our land. In addition to crafting an improved cross as a memorial, Father also named our lane after the presumed deceased. I admired him for always going the extra mile.

As the town grew into a city, the street in Lawrence that runs directly into our lane was also named Somerset. I often imagined how wonderful it would be if the Somerset family traveled through Lawrence and discovered their legacy.

My eyes began to focus as my mind shifted back to the present. I could hardly contain myself as Father turned the wagon onto Somerset Lane. For some reason I was nervous, as if I were about to meet strangers. But as soon I looked through the trees in the lane and saw our family's house, my heart shouted, "I'm finally home!"

I had no idea how uplifting it would be to see my mother's face again. Raymond—who was three years younger than me, and two years older than Jordan—had been sitting watch as we began rolling down the lane.

Even from a distance I could tell that he had grown nearly as tall as Father. I couldn't miss him as he jumped up and ran to the house. Next, I saw Raymond, Jordan, and Mother burst out of the house. All three came running down the lane as I jumped off the wagon and ran to meet them. I nearly knocked Mother over as I picked her up and hugged her, twirling her around in the air. Mother was now the shortest in the family, and six years had blessed her with even more of a glow. With her slightly gray hair in a bun, and an apron dusted with flour, she was the sweetest and most wonderful mother on the face of the earth.

As I set her down, she grabbed my face and kissed me hard on the cheek at least a half dozen times. Raymond and Jordan were both trying to hug me while patting me on the back at the same time. Father stopped the wagon in front of the house and called for Raymond to help him unload my things.

"I can't believe it! I just can't believe it! You're finally home!"

"I can't believe it either, Mom," I said as I gave her another long hug. "Where's Grandfather?"

I was named after my grandfather and father. My first name came from Grandfather, and my middle name was the same as my father's middle name. As much as I loved and admired my father, I was glad I wasn't named Lucius after him.

"He's visiting your grandmother's grave in Pioneer Cemetery. He'll be home soon. Come in the house, Joshua, I want to hear all about college."

"I will, Mom. But first I want to ride over to the cemetery and be with grandpa."

"Oh Joshua," Mother held onto my arm, "I haven't seen you for six years, son. But I know you need to speak to your grandfather, so I won't be selfish. Just don't be long. We didn't kill a fatted calf, but we did kill a fatted hog. It will be ready in less than an hour."

"Yes, ma'am. I won't be long." I gave her another hug.

I was away at school when my grandmother died, and felt guilty that I wasn't at home. She had been ill on and off for almost a year when I left. Up until that period of time, she had always been strong and healthy. Our family rarely got sick, and if we did become ill, we were usually back on our feet rather quickly. We all assumed that whatever illness was trying to take hold would pass, and she would be strong again. Her death came as a shock to us all. She and my grandfather had been married fifty years when she died. I was thankful that both of them had lived long past the average age of our time. Together they had experienced many things while walking arm in arm through good times and bad.

As I rode off to see my grandfather, I remembered witnessing the first burial at Pioneer Cemetery. It was a beautiful and peaceful spot in a field just outside the city on the west side of Lawrence. I had been there a few times before leaving for college, and in my mind it was still largely an empty field. As I got off my horse at the edge of the cemetery, I was astonished at how six years could furnish so many headstones and wooden crosses. There was Grandfather—standing in front of a small white headstone with his hat off and his head bowed. My heart ached for him. After tying my horse to a tree limb, I walked quietly toward the grave. I could see it clearly as I approached: Louise Cole, Beloved Wife— 1790-1857.

Grandfather was one of the two men in my life I admired most. He was gentle, patient, and kind. Father inherited his height and broad shoulders from Grandfather. He also had big strong hands like my father, and gray hair. Grandfather was wise. It seemed as though he could do anything from shoeing and breaking horses to building a house or a barn. He could answer all your questions, bind your wounds, and settle any disputes. He was also one of the bravest men I've ever known. Both my father and grandfather had been in several skirmishes with pro-slavery bandits, although they never spoke of whether or not they had killed anyone. To them, there was no valor in killing another man, nor was there any honor in the campfire tales that followed. Grandfather said once, "It is unfortunate that wicked men have to die without knowing repentance."

As I came near to the grave, I stepped on a twig and Grandfather turned around startled.

"Joshua!" he shouted.

I walked the last few steps in a hurry and gave him a long hug. I could tell he had been crying.

"Grandpa, I'm so sorry I wasn't here when Grandma died. My heart and my prayers were with you."

"Don't worry, Joshua. I understand why you weren't here, and there's nothing you could have done anyway. I've lost track of time. Your mother is probably waiting for us. We better get going."

"Can I stay here with you for a little while longer, Grandpa? The food can wait."

"I'd like that." My grandpa put his arm around me, one of his big hands resting on my shoulder.

We stood silently by the lonely grave for a minutes or so. I longed to offer some great wor fort, yet, there are times in life where there nothing you can say, and it's best that you don't try. Those are the moments when any words you speak will seem shallow and inadequate. Just being with Grandpa was enough. We both understood that.

With a warm summer breeze blowing across my cheek carrying the aroma of a home-cooked meal, I had a deep feeling of contentment as Grandfather and I talked while walking our horses down the lane. As much as I love a summer breeze and the smell of mother's cooking, they fall short of the sense of security and warmth life brings when one spends time with a grandparent. I could say anything to Grandfather without being reproached.

As I was sharing some of my innermost thoughts with him, in the back of my mind I was analyzing how he accomplished his grandfatherly disposition. How could he listen to me share about my shortcomings, and then with so few words and without condoning sin or failure lift my spirit to a place of joy and peace? The only conclusion I could come to at that particular moment was that he gave generously of his time, his warm smile, his listening ear, and his gentle hand on my shoulder. All of these precious gifts were part of a greater storehouse of wisdom that I had not yet attained.

As we walked into the house, Mother said, "You found each other. You're home just in time to eat."

Time to eat! For six long years I had reminisced about my mother's cooking. There was a platter full of pork that came straight from the fire pit in the back yard. Steam was rising, and I could see the juice on the edges of the platter. Father detested dry pork, so he created his own mixture that he used to baste the pork when it was nearly finished cooking. He kept this concoction a secret. All we cared about was how it made the pork tender and juicy. Next to the pork was a bowl full of fresh green beans from the garden with small pieces of ham. Next to this was a plate piled high with fresh sweet corn—everything steaming hot. Mom had baked fresh bread and set out a jar of apple butter. As Grandfather prayed all I could think was, "Please hurry!" I tried my best to be polite while the food was passed. How wonderful it was to be home!

For the moment, we didn't have any runaways in the cellar. Father and Grandfather were the only ones who knew when we would be receiving passengers. This was not an issue of mistrust among the family. They simply didn't want to place the rest of us in any more jeopardy than we already were. They understood if anyone else in the family were threatened or captured, each of us could honestly report that we had no knowledge of when we would be receiving passengers.

After supper we all sat on the porch and shared stories of the last six years. Father told of how bushwhackers (bands of pro-slavery bandits) would threaten or beat abolitionists in the county whenever they had the chance. Mother and I discussed several books that I had studied at Yale, and she told me of the books she had added to her library. Grandfather commented on how wonderful it was that the Pony Express had contracted to extend its service west of Missouri. Raymond and Jordan explained how they had taken over managing the newspaper, and Father talked of how proud he was of Raymond's management ability and Jordan's journalism skills.

Raymond and Jordan had become well-respected in their own right as a businessman and a reporter. A few of Jordan's articles and editorials had even been picked up by a Topeka newspaper. Not only had the town grown up, but so had my brothers. We had become strong and established. Despite the war, our family was doing well and was focused on doing what was good and necessary. I was not only glad to be home, I was proud to be part of such a wonderful heritage.

Answering the Call

The Old School Presbyterian Church (for which I assumed the responsibilities) was organized in 1858 by Reverend William Wilson. For the past year it had been without a minister as Reverend Wilson had joined the Union Army and traveled east to join an artillery regiment in Ohio where his brothers served as officers. There were twenty-five members when the church was first organized, and when I arrived the number had grown to nearly fifty. Our congregation included many local businessmen and influential citizens of Lawrence—Father and Grandfather among them. Reverend Wilson had also set aside one week each month to visit folks in several small settlements outside of Lawrence. I knew my life was about to become very busy with the church in Lawrence, the monthly circuit, and helping my family both at home and at the newspaper.

I had been at Yale two years when the church was organized, so I only knew Reverend Wilson from my parent's letters, but I knew that he was held in high regard by his parishioners. I understood him to be a man of character, courage, and wisdom. I also understood that it would take some time to gain the same level of trust and respect. Father told me something, however, that I thought might work to my advantage. Apparently, the laity had been taking turns filling the pulpit for nearly a year before my arrival. Judging by my father's comments, it seemed rather evident that none of them were called to preach.

Our denomination loved its formality and structure. I subscribed to the truth that wisdom obtains wise counsel, but I also discovered that wise counsel could easily be seduced by the allure of power. During my years at college I was privy to many horror stories of church splits, church takeovers, and pastor's reputations being destroyed by false accusations. Those thoughts made me thankful that father was one of six elders at Old School Presbyterian. I knew he would do his best to look out for my well-being while trying not to step on my toes. He filled me in on some important issues as we walked to my first elder's meeting.

"Joshua, you need to know a couple things before you meet with the rest of the elders. This is not gossip. I'm simply telling you these things because you're my son, and I don't want you going into your first meeting blind."

"Thanks. I'm interested to know what I can expect."

"One thing you need to be aware of is that some of the elders are skeptical of you. What I mean is they can't understand why a graduate of Yale College would desire to preach at a church like ours. Wes Varner recommended you, and Colonel Eldridge seconded the motion. I was certainly in favor of you coming here, but I felt as though

I needed to keep quiet and let the others decide. The other elders went along with it, but I found out later they didn't expect you to answer the call. Several of the elders figured you would decide to stay in the East amongst all the 'educated' people. I've tried to explain to them how we view education."

"Pop, you know I don't look down my nose at anyone! I get sick to my stomach when I'm around educated snobs!"

"Yes, I know that, son. We've talked many times about the value of education, and how a person can use it to help others improve their lives. We understand that education doesn't make a man more valuable or important in God's eyes—it's simply a tool to use to be a blessing to others. Yet, for some reason the elders here are a little suspicious. A lot of their suspicions may just be a result of the times we're living in. Folks are always on the lookout for traitors or thieves. There have been a lot of so-called ministers come through that have taken advantage of people. Even if it's just their insecurities, it's still something you need to be aware of."

"Thanks, Pop," I replied. "I'll be as down-to-earth as I can, and you know that I'll walk with integrity."

"There's one other thing you need to know. They're probably going to recommend not visiting the homesteaders in the outlying areas like Reverend Wilson did. My advice to you is: Speak from your heart, and remember that you're the pastor of the church."

"Well…how ironic! They assume that I'm looking down my nose at them, and yet they think the poor country homesteaders are not worth visiting!"

"Be careful, Joshua." Father gave me a look that let me know I had gone too far. "Use wisdom. Speak the truth, but always do it in love."

"Joshua, you remember Robert Killion, Colonel Eldridge, Jim Grayson, John Lykins, and Wes Varner?"

"It's been awhile, but yes, I remember each of you," I replied as I shook their hands. "A few of us spent quite a bit of time together cutting trees, hauling lumber, and hammering nails. It's good to see all of you!"

Wes Varner spoke for the rest as he said, "On behalf of all the elders of Old School Presbyterian Church, we want to welcome you, Reverend Cole. And may I say that we are very proud to have you back as part of our community."

"Thank you. That means a lot to me, and may I say that it's wonderful to be home."

As we all sat down, Wes called the meeting to order. Other than Father, Wes was the elder I knew the best. He and Father were close, as were our families. Wes was humble, a gentleman, and he always exuded common sense and wisdom. I was glad to have him as the head of the board of elders. He was also an influential business-man, owning a sawmill and a small trading post on the edge of town, as well as several other small businesses. I admired his generosity toward the struggling settlers. Most of them were too proud to accept anything for free, and they didn't have many items of value to trade. So Wes would trade nearly anything they had in order to help them—everything from rusty old pots to arrowheads children found on the trails. I was convinced he had an old shed somewhere full of items he had no use for, items he took in trade in order to provide settlers with food and clothing.

Much of the church business we discussed seemed routine, including a picnic supper to take place the following Saturday as an opportunity for me to really meet my parishioners. Then they discussed the compensation for my service. I expressed that I did not need a salary at that particular time, and that there seemed to be more pressing needs. However, they insisted that some compensation be offered. After offering a gracious objection, and then thanking the elders for their kindness, Father and I dismissed ourselves from the room while the board voted on the issue.

After rejoining the meeting, and just when I thought I had made it through my first elder's meeting unscathed, Wes asked if there was any further business. John Lykins spoke up and said, "About the country settlers, Reverend Cole. My feeling is that it would be more prudent to spend your time ministering here in our community. It's also my feeling that since most of them travel here to trade at least once a month, I think they should also make the effort to attend church here once a month. Anyway, you know as well as I do they'll never be tithing members of our church."

I could feel the tension invade the room as the meeting took a noticeably ugly turn. It wasn't the subject matter that was ugly, or not worth discussing. It was the tone in John Lykin's voice. To be quite frank, I thought his attitude was way out of line for an elder's meeting.

The board's secretary, Robert Killion, began scribbling frantically in the minutes as he tried to accurately record everything that was spoken.

I didn't speak up right away. I remembered Father telling me once that wisdom allows all the voices to speak—whether wise or foolish—and then as delicately as an expert woodcarver, cuts away the ignorance and speaks for itself. John was the only board member I didn't know very well. I knew he was a local banker, which explains why he was so concerned about the settlers giving money to the church. I couldn't put my finger on it at the time, but something deeper about him bothered me.

There was a short pause, which allowed Robert to catch up with the discussion, and then Colonel Eldridge spoke up. "I don't fully agree with everything John said, and I certainly don't approve of his tone. But I do know that many of the settlers have their own religion. Some are Mennonite Brethren, some are Free Methodist, and there are even some who are still Quakers. Some of them have no religion at all. It seems to me that a minister would have to spend a great deal of time trying to bring them into Presbyterianism—much more time then a simple once-a-month visit.

"It might also prove to be an enormous frustration," he continued, "given the fact that the vast majority of them are so uneducated, it almost makes any attempt seem futile. However, my biggest concern, Reverend, is for your safety while traveling. We all recognize that these are dangerous times, especially in the outlying regions."

The colonel was a colorful and complex man. He and his brother had built the first hotel in Lawrence, the Eldridge House. This building was nearly destroyed during the Missouri-Kansas border wars of the late 1850s. I was attending Yale at the time. The Eldridge brothers were not only tough, but also very stubborn. They immediately rebuilt the hotel.

Colonel Eldridge was also a commander with the Kansas Free State Militia. He was a brave man who was constantly involved in deployments resulting in minor battles with Missouri border ruffians (small bands of hard-fisted drifters who would intimidate and raid abolitionist towns). And he was a forceful and opinionated man which I didn't mind. I enjoyed being around men like the colonel. If I were to choose someone to help defend the citizens of Lawrence and the surrounding territory, he would certainly be the obvious choice.

I also enjoyed the colonel's resourcefulness. Recently he arranged for rifles to be shipped from New England to the church in boxes marked "Bibles." To the abolitionists they became known as "Beecher's Bibles" in reference to a statement by Reverend Henry Ward Beecher, a Brooklyn clergyman, who said, "There might be spots where a gun is more useful than a Bible." As much as I admired the colonel, I felt as though what he possessed in courage, he lacked in compassion.

I knew where Wes and Father stood. The other two elders, Jim and Robert, briefly voiced their opinions, taking the safe middle ground. While they were concluding their comments, I began to formulate my response. As I glanced around the table I caught Father and Wes looking at each other with slight grins on their faces. I knew that neither one of them was afraid to speak up. I also understood quite well what the looks on their faces meant: It was time for me to stand on my own two feet. They knew that I would, and they waited.

"Gentlemen, I want to you know that I understand your concerns, and I value your opinions. There is truth in what each one of you said. Are many of the settlers unlearned? Yes. Is it possible that they could journey into town at least once a month to attend a service? Yes. My feeling is that they will not attend a service here because they are also very proud. Many of them don't have Sunday clothes. Many of them don't even have decent everyday walking-around clothes. That's why we never see them come any further than Wes' trading post.

"As far as them being unlearned, maybe that's their fault, maybe that's their choice, or maybe it's because we have not reached out enough. Even though they may not be able to supply tithes and offerings, I believe very strongly that it's our duty to help them—simply because we have been given so much. If we only help those who can help us, then we have accomplished nothing. It was Reverend Wilson who said, 'If a Christian does not give aid to a helpless man, then he has not followed the call of Christ.'

"Concerning my safety, I know that all of you would agree—especially you, Colonel—that it's better for a man to die for a righteous cause than to live as a coward. I believe that God will protect me as I do His work. Gentlemen, I wouldn't intentionally cause any strife or division in this church. But I want you to know I feel very strongly that I must continue to visit those who are less fortunate, even if it means giving up this pastorate."

When I finished speaking, it seemed like an hour of silence before anyone spoke. Wes broke the silence. "Just for the record, I want all of you to know that I agree with every word Reverend Cole spoke."

Father spoke up next and said, "Men, you know where I stand."

Robert, Jim, and the colonel noted their concerns for the record, but then agreed that if we were to err, we should err on the side of compassion. John desired that the record reflect his strong objection. The meeting adjourned and I breathed a sigh of relief.

On the way home, my father put his hand on my shoulder and said, "That was a difficult situation, son, and I'm proud of how you handled it—like a Christian gentleman. Continue to walk in wisdom and compassion and you will always do well." I carried those words with me for the rest of my life.

~

Preaching in the pulpit was the easy part, and by and large my parishioners were very receptive. We had too many social concerns, not the least of which was the safety of our families, to squabble over minor church issues. My biggest challenge was visiting the settlers in the outlying region, and helping them feel connected. In one of the desk drawers at the church I found a crudely drawn map showing the location of those whom Reverend Wilson visited regularly. Even though they were accustomed to a minister calling on them, having a new one meant building a relationship all over again.

I treated any settlers who desired to receive ministry from me in the form of communion, Bible study, or prayer the same as I would my other parishioners—as if they were part of Old School Presbyterian Church. Yet, some of the families homesteaded as far as twenty miles south of Lawrence. There were at least ten families that only saw another person an average of once a month—that person was usually me. This was part of the quandary of helping them feel connected.

Other difficulties arose as I visited the settlers. Even though most of the families I visited were cordial, I found two major stumbling blocks—the biggest one being pride which will manifest itself in many ways. For instance, I always took a small supply of food for myself so I wouldn't be a burden to any family. My plan was to visit during the day and then camp and eat from my supply in the evening. However, many folks were too proud to admit they couldn't afford to feed a visitor. So often during my first trip on the circuit I would enter a friendly tug-of-war over whether or not I should stay and eat supper. If I turned them down, knowing they didn't have extra, I might offend them. On the other hand, I felt guilty if I ate their food.

I encountered another stumbling block when I tried to keep the settlers updated on the war and the current events in Lawrence. They were all interested to know who was winning the war, and how active the Confederate guerillas were in the Lawrence area. The first time I rode the circuit, I made the mistake of taking along several copies of our newspaper. I knew that some of the settlers were unlearned, but I had no concept of how widespread the illiteracy really was. I continually reminded myself of the prophet Zechariah's words: "For who has despised the day of small things?" It was essential to fix my eyes on even the slightest amount of progress.

The first month I visited, I didn't turn down a meal, and I embarrassed the vast majority of families as I suggested reading the newspaper to them. The second month I only ate with half of the settlers, and I only took one newspaper just in case anyone might ask me to read it. By the third month I had officiated at a wedding and a funeral, supplied food for several families (which they gratefully received), and was asked by four families to recite the news. Overall however, I still sensed a noticeable resistance because I was a new minister. It would take time to build their trust.

Like fathers, ministers should not have favorites amongst their parishioners. He must do his best to love everyone equally, and respond to the needs of the rich, the poor, and everyone in between without partiality. But I must confess that one of the pioneer families touched my heart so much it caused me to reach out to them in special ways.

The Higgins family had moved to Kansas as the shadow of the Civil War began to move rapidly across the country. Even though they were white folks, they had worked as laborers for a wealthy plantation owner in southern Kentucky. They became devoted abolitionists after witnessing firsthand the atrocities that had been laid across the backs of the slaves.

In the summer of 1859, in the middle of the night, Jake and Sue Ellen Higgins took their only horse, loaded it with their meager belongings, and, carrying their two small children, began their journey to Kansas. Anyone who met them on their journey could see they were in desperate need. As a result they received a great deal of help along the way. When they finally reached Lawrence, they applied as homesteaders and received thirty acres south of Lawrence. They were thrilled to receive such a large parcel of land.

I nearly wept the first time I rode up to Jake and Sue Ellen's cabin. The acreage Jake was given was thick with woods, briar patches, and marshy ground near a low area of the Kansas River. Most homesteaders would have gone back to the County Land Office and complained until they were granted a different tract. Not Jake. One time I asked him why he didn't protest. He smiled and told me, "I just know there's a reason the good Lord wants me to have this land."

Jake and Sue Ellen had a six-year-old son Rance and an eight-year-old daughter Charlotte. Jake was big and strong, but without another strong male helping him, progress on his land was extremely slow. They had been there nearly three years, but their cabin still resembled a lean-to. Sue Ellen looked absolutely worn out, but like Jake, she smiled and thanked God for the little they had. Jake had cleared a tiny grove of trees and managed to plant a small garden.

Even though they had four chickens, two horses, and one milk cow, for the life of me I could not fathom how they had survived. Their meals consisted of whatever Jake could trap in the river or woods, and the small amount of vegetables and greens they could find or grow. They cooked in a big iron pot over a large fire near their pitiful cabin, looking more like Indians than pioneers.

Despite their dire situation, the Higgins family was the nicest and the most honest and friendly of all the settlers. I had never met a poor family that had such a genuine love for God. They didn't know the Bible well, but I could see that they prayed and trusted God with sincere hearts and a childlike faith. I was surprised to learn that they were one of the most educated families. Amongst the settlers, if you had any schooling at all, you were considered somewhat educated. I learned that while they were living on the plantation, they were taught to read and write.

So often I was struck by the contrast among the pioneer families. Some were uneducated when it came to reading, writing, and arithmetic, but were very industrious farmers and had knowledge of such things from building cabins to breeding livestock. Many of the families who seemed to be doing well were not the friendliest, and often had very little interest in the Lord. In contrast, the Higgins family was the poorest and most unkempt of all the pioneers, yet they were the friendliest, they could read and write, and they had the most enthusiasm for the Lord. They had very few changes of clothing, and their children always looked as though they needed a good scrubbing.

After my first visit at the Higgins place, the Lord reminded me of Hosea 4:6 which says: "My people are destroyed for lack of knowledge." I understood the spiritual application of this passage. And after meeting Jake and Sue Ellen, I also understood how folks will not progress in their everyday lives if they do not have proper knowledge of basic life skills. Though Jake was strong and willing, he had never been taught how to build a proper structure, where to plant a productive field, or how to tackle the most difficult of all tasks—how to make full use of the horrible piece of ground he had been granted. Jake could shoe a horse well, but he had no idea which horses were better than others. He could plow a field well, but he planted his garden in a terrible location that received a miniscule amount of sunlight. Jake and Sue Ellen had the same problem as most of the runaway slaves we helped. All of his life Jake had followed the orders of others, but never assimilated what they were telling him for his own life.

Thankfully, Sue Ellen and Jake had teachable spirits and were eager to learn. If I suggested ways to keep themselves clean and free from disease, they did not take offense. Simple things such as keeping their rain barrel covered so that bugs wouldn't get in and birds didn't deposit their filth into the drinking water. I brought them another iron pot and a large kettle to boil their bathwater in, rather than boiling it in the same pot they cooked food in.

They wanted to know everything they could in order to succeed as homesteaders and, most of all, as Christians. They only needed someone to spend time teaching them. Over a three month period I brought Jake a few simple tools to help cut lumber and drill holes for pegs, and gave him instructions on how to build simple but solid structures. He was like a sponge soaking up every word. A willing pupil is all a teacher requires. I would pour out everything I knew to help someone who was willing to learn, and without a doubt Jake and Sue Ellen desired to learn.

Within a few months worth of visits I watched as Sue Ellen began to take more pride in her family's cleanliness, and I was amazed at how Jake began to improve the condition of their cabin. The best part was, they were excited. Small amounts of progress generated greater enthusiasm in my soul. In the future I saw myself carrying school materials so that I could help teach the parents who, in turn, would hopefully teach their children. I also had an idea how Old School Presbyterian could help supply an immediate need of the settlers. I just knew my congregation would be enthusiastic!

"I hate to sound uncompassionate, Reverend Cole, but you might be moving a little too fast," Wes said as he shook my hand after the Sunday service. "It might be wise to give it a little more time."

I could imagine John Lykins taking that stance, but Wes Varner's words really took me back. I had posted a notice in the vestibule of church stating that we would accept clothing items to give the settlers. I had no idea what an uproar it would cause.

My parishioners had become accustomed to the idea of me visiting the pioneer families. After all, Reverend Wilson had visited them. My desire was to take it a step further and let them know that our church really cared about them. It was obvious to me as I shook hands after the Sunday service that the majority of my congregation wanted no part of it. I looked at my father with disappointment as he came out. "We'll talk on the way home, son," he told me.

"Pop, I don't understand it. I was sure it was the right thing to do. I'm curious how these folks can be abolitionists, yet not even care about those in their own backyard!"

My father listened until I finished ranting, and then began one of his long speeches. His words always put me back on the right path.

"People are funny, son. I've watched and listened to them as the town has grown. When we first settled here, we took all the help we could get. The more the town grew, the more self-sufficient we became. Then we no longer needed or desired the help of an outsider. Pride set in, and we lost sight of those who were truly in need. We figured they could pull themselves up the same way we did, convincing ourselves it's better that way. Besides, the settlers are too proud to accept our help—therefore, it's right for both of us to ignore one another.

"Right now we have nearly half of a nation that's convinced it's morally acceptable to own people as property—no different than a house, a horse, or a plow. People can be wrong, and they can be blinded.

"I agree with what you're trying to do, son, but be careful not to put this issue on the same level as slavery. Unlike the slaves, the pioneers have acted of their own free will—no one forced them to homestead land. That doesn't mean we shouldn't help them whenever we can. Be patient with your congregation. Teach them, and disciple them just as Jesus did. Eventually, they'll come around."

I agreed with what Father said, but it was still difficult to understand why the congregation wasn't more considerate. More and more I realized that small beginnings have as much to do with attitudes of the heart as with material things. I was also reminded that in answering the call to ministry, I had not only come home to the frontlines of abolitionism, but also ignorance, poverty, and hypocrisy. I considered what my father said—to teach and disciple as Jesus did. His words challenged me to re-read the Gospels and rediscover how Jesus dealt with all these attitudes. How did He deal with the multitudes?

How did He deal with the religious leaders? How did He deal with government officials? How did He deal with those closest to Him? After being invigorated by Jesus' life and ministry, I had a renewed determination to be as patient with my congregation as I was with the settlers.

People themselves would become one of my greatest fascinations. They are a wonderful mystery that only the Word of God can solve, or a puzzle that only the Lord can set in order piece-by-piece. We are all different, yet we are all the same. I could put five seemingly different people on display—a rich man, a poor man, an educated man, a king, and a scoundrel. What I would discover is that pride is still pride and prejudice is still prejudice. More than ever it became clear to me that the outward man can be deceiving, and that sin is a matter of the heart—the inner man.

The challenge I faced every morning was to allow the Lord to begin with me, to change my heart. Soon I would discover that there were dark areas of my heart that the Lord would allow to be uncovered, even though I would have preferred that they remain hidden. Yet, my heart would be purged through the fiery trials—trials I would not have endured if it were not for the grace and mercy of the Almighty.

Breaking the Bread of Friendship

*I*t had been over a year since I returned home. I thought about Elisabeth often, and a trip to Topeka was constantly on my mind. I remembered the promise I made to myself that I would visit her one day and apologize for behaving so rudely during the train ride home. However, as a result of settling in, getting started in ministry, helping out at home and at the newspaper, it seemed like the opportunity would never present itself. The day finally came when I had the money and the time.

The night before my trip, my father and I stayed up past sunset talking about courtship and marriage.

"You seem a little nervous, son," he said with a playful look on his face. "Don't you like the idea of meeting the woman God has for you?"

"How will I know who the right woman is?"

"The first place to begin is prayer. Have you prayed about it?"

"I have prayed about it, Pop, but I haven't received any answers."

"The purpose of prayer isn't so we can receive the answers right now. Prayer helps prepare the way. It helps light the path. Prayer helps prepare your heart and hers…whoever she might be. It gives the Lord access to our lives so He can speak clearly when the time is right. Joshua, I believe with all my heart that if you've prayed and given it to the Lord, at the proper time you'll know whether Elisabeth is the one you should court."

"I know one thing—I know how I feel when I think about her."

"You know, son, feelings are certainly a part of love. God made us that way. What did Adam say when he saw Eve for the first time? He said, 'This is now bone of my bone, and flesh of my flesh!' You'll find yourself physically attracted to the one you desire to marry. But the most important part of courtship and marriage is the spiritual aspect. Love's feelings will come and go—even during courtship. Being committed to biblical love, purity, and faithfulness is what creates a solid foundation for marriage. That's part of what proper courtship is all about.

"The truth is, you might think you know what she believes about God. However, there needs to be plenty of discussion about the Lord. Joshua, I've seen couples get married too quickly, and then afterward they discover many of their biblical beliefs are almost opposite. That can cause some awful situations within the marriage relationship. For instance, if a married couple realizes that some of their most cherished beliefs are conflicting, then where do you go to church? How do you raise your children? A proper time of courtship allows you to discuss and pray about these things before you marry. I'm confident that if you'll honor her, honor her parents, and be committed to prayer and purity, the Lord will honor your faith and obedience, and He will guide your steps."

Father's advice was excellent. It was also overwhelming. Was I ready for courtship, or should I simply apologize to Elisabeth and then come back home. Maybe all my thoughts of courtship were not only premature, but could wind up being just another daydream. Was she spoken for? Was she married? Worse yet, would she see me and only be reminded of our last conversation? I would find out soon enough.

I rode off early in the morning for Topeka. I had never been there before, so Father gave me directions in the form of easy-to-follow landmarks. It was only a twenty-five mile trip, and at a leisurely pace took about three hours. On the ride over I prepared my heart for what I might find. I tried to convince myself that this journey was simply a fulfillment of a basic obligation to set right a wrongful act on my part. I didn't want to get my hopes up only to be disappointed.

When I arrived in Topeka, I inquired of a man standing outside a barbershop as to the location of the largest Free Methodist Church in the city. After receiving directions, I rode toward the west side of the city and found a church with a sign that read: Topeka Free Methodist Church—Rev. Lewis Morgan. Obviously I had the correct church, but I still didn't know where the family lived.

I took a chance and knocked on the door to the house next to the church assuming it might be the parsonage. A tall, middle-aged man answered the door.

As I reached out my hand to shake his, I asked, "Are you Reverend Morgan?"

"I am."

"Sir, I'm Joshua Cole of Lawrence..."

Before I could explain why I had come, he grabbed my hand, pulled me into the house, and patted me on the back several times. "Welcome, Joshua! I have been anxious to meet you!"

Surprised, I said, "It's nice to meet you too, sir, but how did you know about me?"

"Elisabeth told me about meeting you on the train. Since then the Lord has put you on my heart many times. I want you to know that I've been praying for you and your ministry in Lawrence. Come and sit down in the parlor. I want to hear all about what the Lord's doing in your life."

It felt good to know that Elisabeth had mentioned me to her father. That caused me to wonder how often she thought of me, and if she would be excited to see me. These thoughts made me a little nervous, but also increased my desire to see her again.

The parsonage was not very large, but it was warm and inviting. Reverend Morgan's outgoing nature quickly put me at ease. Almost immediately I felt as comfortable with him as I did with my own father. He was nearly as tall as my father, and his dark hair was turning slightly gray. He spoke with a jovial, but authoritative, voice.

As we sat down, Reverend Morgan said, "Before I call Elisabeth, tell me how you and your church are doing."

"Well sir, it's taken a little time to get to know the congregation, but it seems as though they're getting comfortable with me. If I can be frank with you, one of my biggest frustrations is that they seem to only respond to sermons with an abolitionist theme. I have a desire to preach about so many other important topics, but if I veer too far, it's almost as if they become bored."

"That's a tough one, Joshua. I'll be praying about that. As ministers we can't force folks to go where they're not ready or equipped to go. On the other hand, that's the primary part of our calling—to equip the saints. We can pray that the Lord will give you creative ways to weave a theme of freedom within those other important topics."

I was so taken back by Reverend Morgan's interest in my church and pastorate, and by his eagerness to pray for me, that I didn't hear Elisabeth entering the parlor behind the chair where I was sitting.

"Joshua!" We stood as Elisabeth entered the parlor. Reverend Morgan smiled at her as she went on to say, "I'm so glad you're here!"

She was even more beautiful than I remembered. For the life of me I cannot recall what I said, or whether or not my mouth dropped open, as she gracefully walked into the room and gave me a modest embrace.

"Please sit down," she said.

I managed to mumble a simple hello, and then I sat back down.

When we were all seated, Elisabeth continued, "What a wonderful surprise! I've been praying that we would meet again someday. When I returned home last year I told Mother and Father all about you, and how you were taking a church in Lawrence."

Before the conversation continued, I needed to explain to Elisabeth the reason I had come.

"Before we talk about anything else, Elisabeth, I feel that I must apologize for my rude behavior the last time we met." I fumbled over my words. "It's something that has bothered me greatly. I honestly didn't know whether you would even speak to me again after how I acted on the train. I realize that it's been a year since we first met. I was a little concerned you might be spoken for, in which case my visit wouldn't be appropriate and I should apologize and say good day. In any case, I just wanted you to know that I'm very sorry, and I hope you will accept my sincere apology."

"Joshua, I do accept your apology. But there is really no need. I was the one who was rude. I could see that you were very tired that day, and I kept pressing for more conversation. That was wrong. I was concerned that you would always remember me as being too impetuous or impolite. And no...I'm not spoken for." She spoke timidly as her father raised an inquisitive eyebrow.

I felt as though I had embarrassed Elisabeth, so I tried to move the conversation away from the talk of courtship.

"I got concerned when I didn't see you get off the train in St. Louis," I said curiously. "I was sure that I had offended you."

"Oh, that's not at all what happened. I was enjoying our conversation about the Lord so much that I forgot to mention I was getting off in Illinois to stay with an aunt for a few days. You were sound asleep when the train stopped to let off passengers, and I didn't want to wake you. But, I assure you, I was not offended."

I was so relieved! A tremendous burden had been lifted from me. I was also delighted that Elisabeth did not have a suitor. Was it possible that a doorway had just opened in my life? Suddenly I felt an excitement in my heart about the possibility of getting to know one another. Is this the answer that Father and I discussed? One part of me felt like rushing in, but I knew that wisdom would say take it slowly.

For the next two hours the three of us discussed life in Kansas, the war, and the importance of being ministers in such perilous times. Our time together passed quickly, and I savored every moment. I didn't realize how much I needed to get away for a day or two. It was encouraging to be able to discuss ministry with Elisabeth's father without the fear of someone in my congregation thinking I was complaining. Any minister who is not simply a "hireling" loves his congregation, but also needs a break now and then. Otherwise, he may find himself becoming frustrated, or even callous, toward the very people the Lord has called him to love and care for. I was enjoying our conversation so much that I lost track of time.

"Have I been here two hours?" I asked surprised. "I really should be going. I feel as though I've taken advantage of your time and hospitality."

"Nonsense, Joshua, you don't have to rush off," Reverend Morgan said. "But if you have to go, then why not come back this evening and have supper with us? My wife Gloria is visiting a friend right now, but if you come back you can meet her as well."

"Well sir, I was prepared to stay overnight in a hotel just in case I had trouble finding you."

"Wonderful! Gloria would love to meet you. But we'll take it one thing at a time. First, let's put your horse in the barn and get him some feed. After that Elisabeth and I will walk you to the hotel so you can get settled in. It's not very far."

The Morgans had a small barn in the rear of their house with several horses and a nice looking black, four-seat buggy. Elisabeth introduced me to her horse Charlemagne—a beautiful white Appaloosa with black spots. Impressed, I commented, "I feel funny putting my plain brown workhorse in a barn with such a beautiful animal."

"Oh, he's just a big baby," Elisabeth said as she stroked Charlemagne's neck. "He'll appreciate the company."

"I can see you love horses. I assume you also enjoy riding."

"Oh yes. There's nothing like riding out into the fields on a sunny day and spending time with the Lord."

"Maybe with your parents' permission we might enjoy a ride together sometime."

Before Elisabeth could respond, Reverend Morgan said, "We're all set here. Now we'll take you to the hotel."

As we walked along, I couldn't help but try to identify what made Elisabeth so different. By all standards, she and her family were common, ordinary people. Even though her outward appearance was unmistakably attractive, and even though this was only our second meeting, I could already see that she possessed an inward beauty that far exceeded anything I had ever encountered. I wondered what caused this beauty to shine through so clearly. I also wondered if she had any idea of the thoughts streaming through my mind as I walked with her and her father.

As my mind churned, I came to the realization that it was the overflow of her genuine love for God and the purity of her heart that accentuated her outward beauty. When I lived in the East, I discovered that the words of Petrarch rang true: "Rarely do great beauty and great virtue dwell together." This was not the case with Elisabeth. When I walked beside her, I felt in the presence of nobility.

"Here we are, Joshua." Reverend Morgan broke into my thoughts. "I'd suggest taking some time to get settled in the hotel, and rest a while. You know as well as I do that ministers rarely have that opportunity. And plan on coming to the house for supper. We'll eat around five o'clock."

"I'll be there."

Reverend Morgan was right. I needed a good rest.

⟶

"Mrs. Morgan, that was absolutely delicious!" I said as I wiped my mouth with a napkin.

"Thank you, Joshua. These dishes can wait until later. Why don't we all go into the parlor and have some coffee?"

"Great idea, Gloria," her husband responded. "What's for dessert?"

"Your daughter made an apple pie. You all relax, and I'll get it." Mrs. Morgan walked into the kitchen.

As we sat down, Reverend Morgan said, "Joshua, tell me about Yale and your studies there. Six years of biblical study? That must have been intense. And what made you desire to attend Yale?"

"Well sir, I've always enjoyed learning, and the Bible has always fascinated me the most," I explained. "My parents were both educated in the East, and my father attended Yale College. They made sure my brothers and I had the finest education offered. What I mean is, our education occurred at home. Mother taught us, and she saw to it that we studied and understood what we learned. Back East, Father worked for a man named Amos Lawrence."

"That's who your city is named after?"

"Yes sir, that's correct. Amos is an old family friend. He and my grandfather were very close. Father was running one of his textile mills when Amos asked him to lead a company of pioneers to Kansas. I was a teenager at the time, and I had already expressed a desire to attend Yale. I never mentioned it again after plans were made to head west, but Father never forgot my desire. I didn't know it until we were here for a year, but Amos had already made arrangements for me to attend Yale, and even paid for my tuition and books. The only expense I incurred was for my room and board. Amos could have easily paid for that as well, but they both thought it was a good idea that I work and pay for a portion of my expenses. So, my roommate and I worked at the New Haven shipyards during the summer. That was an education in and of itself."

"My goodness, the Lord has really made the way for you! What a tremendous testimony. Tell me about your studies at Yale. Did they take you deeper in your walk with the Lord?"

I was spared from having to answer his question when Mrs. Morgan returned with the pie and coffee. Reverend Morgan stood to help her, and then obviously forgot the question he asked. I was thankful. Deep in my heart, I knew my studies at Yale had provided me with excellent knowledge, but they lacked spiritual depth. After spending this small amount of time with Reverend Morgan and his family, I knew they were spiritual giants in comparison to the majority of those I graduated with at Yale—except Harry, of course.

We visited a while longer while eating pie, drinking coffee, and enjoying each other's company. I was having a wonderful time, but I didn't want to overstay my welcome.

"Thank you for such a nice evening. I should be going," I said as I stood to say good-bye.

Mrs. Morgan smiled warmly. "We've all enjoyed visiting, and it's been nice getting to know you better, Joshua. Are you going to be in town tomorrow as well?"

"Yes, ma'am. I'll leave tomorrow afternoon."

As the Morgans walked me to the door, Reverend Morgan patted me on the back and said, "Don't be a stranger, Joshua, now that you know where we live."

As I left the house and began walking down the street, I turned to see Elisabeth standing in the doorway. I waved and she waved back. My heart felt as though it would leap out of my chest! Elisabeth's family was wonderful. She was wonderful. I thought about her as I lie awake for hours, not being able to sleep. All the extraordinary moments of the day flashed through my mind. I saw her face once again just as it was the moment I turned around in the parlor. I could see her standing next to Charlemagne stroking his mane. I envisioned her elegant manner as she ate dinner, and then for a moment our eyes met.

I wondered if she was thinking about me too. I never imagined on my way to Topeka that I would be pondering thoughts of marriage and family. What would it be like? Was Elisabeth a woman I could spend the rest of my life with? A new door had opened in my life—the door to my heart, which was telling me she was a woman I would consider marrying. I finally went to sleep.

"We thought you might be a little shy about coming to the house, so we decided to come to the hotel," Elisabeth said, her mother and father standing by. "Since this is your last day in town, we were hoping you would accompany us on a picnic."

She was right. I was very anxious to see her, but I didn't want to seem too anxious. I also didn't want to be a bother to her family. A picnic with the Morgans, however, was ideal. I quickly said yes, and we were on our way.

We couldn't have asked for a more beautiful day. There wasn't a cloud in the sky. And even though it was the middle of August, a slight breeze provided relief from the heat. We found the perfect spot about a half mile east of Topeka—a clearing by a small grove of trees. Mrs. Morgan had prepared another delicious meal complete with fried chicken, muffins, and leftover apple pie. We spread a blanket, sat down in the shade, and then joined hands as Reverend Morgan prayed over the meal.

As we ate lunch and visited with one another, I found myself staring directly into Elisabeth's eyes—a brilliant display of the peacefulness and confidence in her heart.

She spoke volumes without saying a word. I knew I could be completely truthful with her—I could bare my soul. I figured I might as well; I was convinced she could see right through me anyway.

After lunch, and a very enjoyable conversation, Reverend and Mrs. Morgan allowed Elisabeth and me to spend some time together alone. Well, almost alone— they were about fifty yards away. The last time we had a conversation of our own, it didn't go well. On this day, however, our conversation was more than pleasant. There were no disputes or theological debates. I let my guard down for the first time, and gave her a glimpse of my soul. Elisabeth responded with sensitivity and joy, and I felt even more that God was knitting our hearts together.

"Joshua, what do you love most about church?"

"I would have to say communion."

"Really? That's wonderful." Elisabeth's eyes lit up, "There's nothing more profound than being reminded of what Jesus has done for us."

"Yes. For me it's that truth, and so much that I cannot put my finger on. Elisabeth, when I sit down after praying over the bread and wine, I never feel more inadequate than at that moment. I know these feelings of inadequacy don't come from the Lord. I'm secure in the knowledge that He has saved me and that I'm His child. Even so, when I consider what He has done for me, I don't even feel worthy to take the elements. Maybe that's it…the overwhelming sense of the grace and mercy of God. To know that without Him we're hopelessly lost. That realization always deepens my commitment to the Lord."

Suddenly I noticed a tear rolling down Elisabeth's cheek.

"Did I say something wrong?"

"No, Joshua. I love what you just said. It touched me deeply."

At that moment I wished I could stop the world and just linger a while—at least long enough to absorb and truly appreciate the fact that words came directly from my heart and touched hers.

The Lord granted us a perfect day. We not only broke bread together, we also broke through a barrier into true friendship. Even though I felt Elisabeth's spiritual life was much deeper than mine, it didn't bother me because it was genuine, and she was not arrogant or condescending. Not only did I cherish the time we spent together, but her love for the Lord was calling me to a deeper walk with Him. She had a soft and gentle way of encouraging me to experience more of God.

"I can't express to you how much I have enjoyed our time together, and I wish today didn't have to end," I said with regret, "but I do need to leave town pretty soon. I'd like to get home before dark."

"Can we pray together before we leave?" Elisabeth asked.

It took a moment for me to respond—an embarrassing moment! I was a minister and I certainly didn't mind praying in front of people—even though most of my prayers were either written out ahead of time, or were routine when I prayed for dinner or over the communion table. But to spontaneously pray together—I was dumbfounded.

I was grateful when Elisabeth went on to say, "Joshua, if you don't mind, I would like to pray for both of us."

Eagerly I said, "Yes, please do."

I listened in awe as Elisabeth prayed from her heart: "Dear Father, You see our hearts. Father, you know our desires and our thoughts. Lord, we ask today for Your wisdom as we continue to get to know each other. Purge our hearts of any evil desires, and grant us Your power to remain pure. Guide our thoughts. We love you so much, Father, and we desire only to follow Your will for our lives. Give our parents wisdom and guidance, and help us to be fully submitted to those in authority over us so that You will be glorified in our lives. We ask this in the name of Your Son Jesus, our Savior, amen."

As Elisabeth finished, I knew how Jesus' disciples must have felt when they heard Him pray. I wanted to echo the disciples' words and say, "Teach me how to pray." Elisabeth and I were so oblivious to the rest of the world, we didn't realize her mother and father were standing beside us as she ended her prayer. My speechlessness was interrupted by Reverend Morgan saying, "Amen. It's time to go."

These were some of the most wonderful moments I had ever experienced. While picnicking with Elisabeth and her family, I completely forgot the country was at war. Nothing existed outside of the happiness that over-whelmed my soul. All of that was about to change.

Quantrill's Raiders

"Bodies of dead men…were laying in all directions."
- *Survivor of the Lawrence Massacre*

"Joshua! Joshua! Lewis, I don't see any wounds. His eyes are open and he's breathing, but I don't think he can hear us."

"Father, he's in shock! We need to get him in the house and put him to bed!"

I heard the voices, but my body was numb. I couldn't move or speak. I didn't know where I was, and I had no recollection of how I got there. I felt completely exhausted—mentally and physically.

Then I recognized Elisabeth's voice as she said; "Lay him down on his bed. Pull his boots off, and put a blanket on him."

"Joshua, do you know who I am?"

"Of course I do…you're Elisabeth Morgan. But what are you doing in our house? And how long have I been asleep?"

"You've slept twelve hours straight. Do you remember anything about what happened here? There was blood on your hands, and dirt all over your pants."

Suddenly all the events of August 21, 1863, came flooding into my mind. I screamed, "Oh Lord, they're all dead!" My body shook, and I began weeping uncontrollably as my mind drifted through the events of the last twenty-four hours.

After the beautiful day with the Morgans, I returned from Topeka just as the sun was going down. The dark clouds in the sky gave a warning of rain, and as I approached the house, I could tell something wasn't right. I didn't see anyone sitting watch in the lane, and there was no activity outside the house which was unusual. All of a sudden I had a sick feeling in my stomach.

In the front and on the side of the house I saw what looked like a couple dozen large lumps of dirt. Then I realized what the "lumps" were. They were people—bodies. I whipped my horse with the reins and rode hard into the front yard.

Leaping off my horse, I stood horrified as I looked at the dirt churned up around the house and the bodies that seemed to be everywhere. The yard looked as though it had been plowed for a spring plant. There must have been over fifty horses kicking their hooves to turn over that much soil. I yelled out, but nobody responded. I grabbed a rifle lying on the ground next to a dead man. I didn't want anyone taking me by surprise.

As I walked closer to the house, I saw what my heart feared the most—my father and grandfather lying on their backs! They were about ten feet apart from each other, and both had rifles in their hands. I ran to my father and knelt down beside him. He was dead. Several bullet holes had stolen his breath, and blood was still fresh on his overalls and nightshirt. Tears and numbness came over me simultaneously as I fell across the lifeless body.

After a few moments I stood and took several slow steps to where my grandfather lay—also lifeless. For a moment I hoped that he would simply wake up, but instead he just stared at me with hollow eyes. Neither Father nor Grandfather had boots on. They had been taken completely by surprise.

There were over a dozen dead bodies in the front and around the side of the house, but I didn't recognize any of the others. As I walked cautiously around to the rear of the house, I found more familiar bodies near the woods: four runaway slaves—a mother, two children, and one man. The mother and two children had obviously been running toward the woods as they were shot in the back. It was plain to see that the murderers were brutal as each victim had been shot multiple times.

The runaways in the rear of the house provided more evidence that my family had been taken by surprise. There was obviously no time to open the tunnel. It was also evident that the male runaway tried to fight his attackers as I found a confederate rifle in his hands. I knew the rifle didn't belong to our family because it had a bayonet fixed on the end and a confederate flag painted on the stock. This brave runaway had either fought his murderers hand-to-hand, or picked up a rifle from the dead and wounded. He was not simply a runaway slave; he was a man willing to face his oppressors and fight for his freedom. All this evidence made me wonder if the Confederate Army had advanced into Kansas. Was I now in the middle of the war?

I took a deep breath as I walked toward the house, not knowing what I would find next. My heart sank further when I found Raymond at one of the hidden cellar doors. He was still clutching the door handle which he had opened to release those in the cellar when he was shot and killed. Raymond had his boots on. He must have been outside doing the early chores as the killers took them by surprise. Judging by the short distance the runaways were able to cover, and the fact that Raymond was still holding the door handle, he must have been in the barn when the shooting began.

My legs began to quiver as I stepped into the rear door of the house and walked slowly through the kitchen and into the parlor. Our front door had been broken down. There were bullet holes everywhere. The mirror over the fireplace was shot to pieces. My knees finally gave out as I looked down and saw my mother lying on the floor clutching her Bible. Her eyes were open and her dress was full of blood. I knelt down over her body and wept.

There were two dead men in the parlor I didn't recognize. I remember screaming in anger, and then dragging both dead men out of the house and throwing them off the front porch into the yard. In my rage it seemed easy— like throwing sacks of grain off the back of a wagon. It also seemed easy to cock the rifle and point it at one of the dead men. I can't explain what made me do it; maybe some desperate need for satisfaction or revenge. When the rifle didn't fire, I threw it at them. At that point, I remember walking to the front porch. I sat on one of the rocking chairs and stared—motionless and detached. After that, there was only a fog until I stepped out of the clouds in my mind and realized Elisabeth and her mother were holding me as I wept.

I must have drifted into another deep sleep. As I awoke, I heard Reverend Morgan at my bedroom door say, "Elisabeth, get your mother. We've got to decide quickly what to do with all these bodies before the August heat and swarming bugs bring disease."

His words caused me to sit straight up in the bed. Suddenly I was reminded again of the events of the past day and a half. Even though I was still numb inside, I knew I had to get up and help make decisions concerning the burial of my family. I looked out the window of my upstairs room, and I could see our wagon in the front of the house with the bodies of my family laid neatly in the rear. Reverend Morgan was covering the bodies with blankets and I saw Elisabeth walking from the wagon toward the side of the house.

As I walked into the parlor, I noticed immediately that many things had been straightened up and cleaned. The Morgans had been working incredibly hard and fast in the last twenty-four hours trying to convert a living nightmare into a bad dream. As Elisabeth and her mother came through the back door, all I could say was, "Thank you all for your kindness."

"Joshua, you may not feel like it, but you need to eat," said Mrs. Morgan. "There's breakfast on the table."

Reverend Morgan walked into the kitchen just as I was sitting down. He put his arm on my shoulder and said, "Get some strength, son, and then we have to talk."

"How did you get here?" I asked faintly. "How did you know where we live?"

"News about the attack spread quickly," Reverend Morgan explained. "We received the news in the middle of the night following the raid. We were very concerned about you and your family, so we got in the buggy and hurried toward Lawrence. We remembered that your house was on the north side of the city, and when we saw the lane with the trees, that's when we knew."

"You took an awful chance in coming here."

"It was a chance we were willing to take. Besides, Joshua, in times like these we're all at risk almost anywhere we go. We couldn't just sit at home and do nothing."

As I sat in the kitchen forcing down a little food, I had no idea how bad the massacre in Lawrence had been. Later, I read an article published just two days after the raid. The *Leavenworth Daily Conservative* headlined the account as follows: "Total Loss $2,000,000, Cash Lost $250,000." The story described the scene along Massachusetts Street, the business artery of Lawrence:

> Lawrence was one mass of smoldering ruins and crumbling walls. Only two business houses were left upon the street—one known as the Armory and the other the old Miller block. About one hundred and twenty-five houses in all were burned, and only one or two escaped being ransacked while everything of value was carried away or destroyed.

The article went on to point out that the offices of three Lawrence newspapers—the *Journal*, *Tribune*, and *Republican*—were destroyed, and that every safe in the town but two had been robbed. Eyewitness accounts also reported that nearly four hundred and fifty bushwhackers were led by a Confederate named William C. Quantrill. Even though Quantrill claimed to be a lieutenant colonel in the Confederate Army, we viewed him as nothing more than a rogue opportunist, who used a Confederate uniform to justify being a thief and a murderer.

As I sat at the kitchen table eating, I suddenly realized that I had not seen the body of my brother Jordan! How could my mind be in such a stupor that I could overlook such a huge detail? I nearly knocked the kitchen table over as I jumped up and ran out the back door, frantically calling Jordan's name and searching for his body. *Is it possible that he's still alive? Did he escape into the woods? Was he in the cellar?*

The Morgans caught up with me as I stopped to catch my breath.

"What's wrong, Joshua? What are you looking for?" Elisabeth shouted.

"My brother Jordan," I said breathing hard. "I can't find him—dead or alive!"

I hollered again, "Jordan! Jordan!"

Reverend Morgan grabbed me by the shoulders. "Joshua, I promise we'll search for Jordan, but first we must take care of your family. You need to tell me where you want them laid to rest. In light of what you're going through, son, I'm very sorry to have to press this issue. But it must be taken care of quickly."

"Pioneer Cemetery, next to my grandmother," was all I could say.

Before we left for the cemetery, I insisted on searching the cellar, the tunnel, and the grounds around the house. There was no sign of Jordan.

Many buildings were still smoldering as we rode through town. I didn't remember seeing any smoke from the fires as I rode back from Topeka that horrible night. Either they must have settled down by the time I rode in, or my mind had been utterly distracted by the memory of a perfect day. I do remember thinking that it looked as though it might rain. Maybe the darkness was created by the smoke. Or, maybe it had already rained and settled the fires. I was tired of trying to figure it all out. I wanted the horror to end. I wanted my family back.

I took a hard look at the people of Lawrence as we rode through town. They looked helpless, hopeless, and utterly forsaken. The destruction was unimaginable. Buildings reduced to rubble. People picking through the ashes. Mothers huddled in the streets with their children, staring at the remains of their homes. My eyes couldn't focus. The dark cruel misery reminded me of a Dickens novel.

The bodies of some of the Confederate raiders were still lying in the streets. Folks spit on them as they walked by. I didn't know—and never desired to know—what Reverend Morgan and his family did with the Confederates who died on my property. We buried the runaway slaves next to the Somerset grave in the rear of the house near the woods. They weren't running anymore—they were finally free.

I felt nothing as I helped Elisabeth's father dig four graves next to my grandmother's. They were all so kind and caring. Mrs. Morgan had put a different dress on Mother so she would be buried with dignity. We then wrapped each of my family members in blankets, and with two ropes Reverend Morgan and I gently lowered them into their graves.

Once again, the dreadful reality sank in as I threw shovels of dirt into my father's grave. Then my knees gave out, and I knelt and sobbed as Elisabeth and her mother picked up the shovel and finished the task. I don't remember any of the words Reverend Morgan spoke at the gravesides. I just remember how we all wept as he read scripture and prayed through his tears. And I remember the unyielding silence as we rode in the wagon back through town, and down Somerset Lane.

The next day Elisabeth's father and I rose early and began searching for Jordan. We combed the woods and the town. We asked everyone we encountered if they had seen him. Other families were also looking for loved ones—mostly in the rubble. Several days of effort turned up nothing. While we had been out searching, Elisabeth and her mother worked hard scrubbing and cleaning, trying to erase the markings of war. It helped, and I was thankful—though the deeper scars would require a more powerful hand than what they could supply. I had not fired a shot, and yet I was thrust deep into battle. I suffered the worst wound of all, the broken heart of a loved one left behind.

As the Morgans prepared to leave, we hugged each other and I thanked them again for all they had done. I owed them a debt I could never repay. Reverend Morgan assured me that he would come and check on me. He understood grief. And he knew that when the numbness wore off and reality set in, those would be some of the most difficult and lonely times. As I watched their buggy disappear into the field, the utter loneliness sunk in. I didn't want them to go. I didn't want to face life without my family. Not only was I grieving, but it seemed that every day following the massacre I dealt with fits of rage. I wanted to shoot something, or hit somebody. No matter how hard I swung the axe chopping wood, or how many times I let out a scream, nothing seemed to satisfy the anger that boiled inside me.

—

I was thankful that my family's house was still intact, even though many items were stolen and a careless attempt was made at setting fire to the beautiful porch that wrapped around from the front to both sides. It was constructed that way on purpose—to create an easy entrance, exit, and vantage point for early warnings. With exception of the eaves, roof, and green shutters, the house was almost entirely brick on the outside. The porch had the usual wooden latticework and wooden decking, but otherwise it had a brick foundation and brick pillars which made arson rather difficult. Even though the structure was relatively unscathed, it would be quite some time before I felt at ease living there. With five bedrooms, a large parlor, a library, kitchen, and dining room, it was a vastly empty and lonely place.

There didn't seem to be any rhyme or reason to Quantrill's plan of attack. Maybe that was the evil fashion in which murder and mayhem always unfolds—random and ruthless. Be that as it may, I continued trying to put the pieces of the puzzle together. I came to the conclusion that Quantrill and his men did not fully understand the role our house and property played within the Underground Railroad. If they had, it seems likely they would have spent more time trying to destroy it. I figured our house was either the last stop for the bandits, or possibly only a portion of them came to the north side of town, and then met the others at the end of their murderous rampage. I wouldn't be surprised if Father and Grandfather hurried them along by killing several of their company.

As I surveyed the loss of property, I further realized how fortunate I was compared to many of the townspeople. While the safe at the newspaper had so many bullet holes in it that it was quite useless, I was thankful our business office was not completely destroyed. Even so, no more newspapers would be published by the *Herald of Freedom*.

Just a few days after the brutal massacre I was told that our mayor, George Cullamore, had received bits and pieces of information warning that Quantrill and his raiders were planning to attack Lawrence. In response, Mayor Cullamore activated the militia and even sent a request to Fort Leavenworth for additional troops and cannons. However, when the troops from Leavenworth were ordered back to the fort, Mayor Cullamore took it as a sign that Lawrence was no longer at risk. Many of the townspeople even felt secure enough to attend a band concert the night before the raid.

As city officials continued to investigate, we learned that a local minister, Reverend Snyder, who lived on East 19th Street, was the first to be murdered. Apparently he was milking a cow when Quantrill's bandits rode in. From the Snyder place Quantrill and his men rode through town burning, killing, and pillaging anything and everything in their path.

I was horrified as I heard firsthand accounts of several close friends and church members. One of my parishioners, R.G. Elliot, told me how he witnessed the murderers riding in around five o'clock in the morning and gunning down unarmed men and women. He described how people surrendered every dollar they had in hopes of saving their lives, only to be shot and killed. With tears in his eyes R.G. said, "Reverend, it was a dreadful sight seeing wounded men lying helpless and dying, while houses and businesses burned in the background."

An old family friend, Judge Bailey, choked back tears as he told me how he went house to house trying to help folks after the raid. The judge said the Eldridge House was already in ruins, along with the County Building and nearly everything on both sides of Massachusetts Street. Then, after going around to Vermont Street, he said he found the Johnson House (another hotel) burned and half a dozen corpses lying just north of it. Near the Johnson House he saw a crowd of women and children making piles on the ground of the few personal items they had been able to snatch from their burning houses.

I was relieved to hear at least one testimony of lives being spared. Hattie Wilcox, another of my parishioners, told me that she plead with Quantrill to spare her and her house. Hattie owns and runs a boarding house—a beautiful brick home on Indiana Street—which looks very similar to ours. After explaining to Quantrill that this was her only source of income, somehow he was able to muster a fly speck of decency, and he spared Hattie and her son who was hiding in the copula at the time.

After speaking with friends and parishioners, a multitude of thoughts raced through my mind as I continued trying to come to grips with all that had happened. How could men do this to one another? How can you point a rifle at a fellow countryman and pull the trigger? How can a man be a hero to some and a murderer to others? Are there times when it is acceptable to hate and even kill? I tried to come up with answers, but I couldn't. What bothered me most was the callousness I felt growing in my own heart.

This hardness worsened as I read another account of the massacre in the *Kansas State Journal*, the first Lawrence newspaper to resume publication following the raid. What I read seemed unthinkable. The article claimed that every business house had been sacked and all but five burned. In addition, every residence in town had been plundered. In essence, the *Journal* portrayed the raid as indiscriminate and brutal. All of this was not news to me. I walked in the nightmare. What I found unbelievable was what the lead article went on to say:

> The question of how such loss of life and destruction of property could come about is not the moot question it once was. There is increasing evidence to support the suspicion that the success of the Quantrill raid was assured by "insiders" who, for personal, political, or economic reasons, stood to gain from the destruction of Lawrence.

Insiders! How could someone I may have known give aid to the murderers who took my family and so many others in Lawrence? This news made me burn with anger. I not only wanted to know who the insiders were, I wanted to see them hang!

As a Christian I had no problem with public executions for those who had been fairly judged for crimes warranting such punishment. When done properly, within due process, these events reassured the public that those committing such crimes would be brought to justice. Furthermore, public hangings served as a compelling visual deterrent for would-be criminals.

Even though I would never argue against swift and judicious punishment for crimes, I would discover that seeing a man hang does not carry with it peace for the soul. Once again, that would take someone infinitely more powerful than any earthly authority.

Oh Wretched Man that I Am

I kept having the same nightmare. I dreamed I was riding frantically toward the house as I saw my family being gunned down by at least a hundred men on horseback. Father was yelling, "Joshua, help us!" By the time I leaped off my horse, they were already dead, all the murderers had disappeared, and I was left standing in a fog. The nightmare caused me to wake up in a cold sweat, my heart pounding and my soul riddled with guilt over not being there for my family. "I should have died with them," I thought.

One particular night, I sat straight up in bed, screaming as loud as I could in the dark empty house. I envisioned myself picking up a rifle and shooting the first Southerner I could find, and then stabbing him repeatedly with the bayonet after he fell to the ground. I didn't care if he was tall or short, slender or large, or even if he had family waiting for him to return home.

What was happening to me? I had never experienced this type of hatred for my fellow man. Each morning when I got out of bed I felt anger charging through every muscle and fiber of my being.

For the most part this anger reared its ugly head only at home. Somehow I managed to keep it hidden from my parishioners which was difficult, given the fact that the majority of my church members had also lost loved ones. Those who hadn't were close to someone who had. I was surrounded with outcries of emotions and constant reminders of the pain we had suffered. Following the massacre, I forced myself to go through the motions as I conducted one funeral service after another.

I felt hypocritical as I comforted my parishioners, knowing I didn't have peace in my own heart. I struggled to answer tough questions and give counsel to others while my own solace was utterly undone. Most of the dead were buried right away, and then services conducted afterward as ministers from several communities volunteered to speak with families and pray at the gravesides. No matter how many prayers, no matter how many tears, we each had a vast emptiness in our souls that only divine intervention could fill.

After all the bodies of the deceased were securely in their graves, the final death toll was one hundred and sixty-four. Forty of Quantrill's men had been killed, and a member of the clergy reluctantly volunteered to say a few words over their large unmarked grave. This difficult chore was a small step, and much was left to do. Nevertheless, after we had buried the dead, it seemed as though we had turned a corner and could move on with our lives.

Yet, how could I move on as if nothing had happened while I was still plagued by so many questions? How can any man's thought processes be so wrong? I wondered. How can a human being believe that it is morally right to enslave other human beings, and then be willing to die for that immoral belief? Why didn't God protect my family as they worked for His righteous cause? Was my heart becoming so hard that I didn't care what was biblically correct? Had I become completely insensitive to the everlasting consequences?

I became angrier as I considered how the Lord could allow me to be cast into such an evil and tumultuous situation. He knew this was in my future, yet He allowed it to happen! According to my beliefs I was predestined for the horrors I had encountered. What was I to do? I was angry at people. I was angry at God. And I was angry at myself for the internal struggle and the feelings that boiled inside of me!

The only thing that helped was to help others. Those in the city, who were fortunate enough to have their homes intact, helped others tear down and haul off the wreckage. Day after day we drove wagons full of burnt wood and rubble to the outskirts of town where we burned everything we could. The process of clearing debris was enormous, and it would take us quite some time to complete.

Old School Presbyterian Church had suffered some damage, but when compared with much of the city it almost looked untouched. Quantrill's men had shot out windows and set fire to the entryway. However, with nothing of great value to steal and no parishioners inside so early in the morning, they certainly hadn't given it much attention. Wes Varner, who lived close to the church, told me later that he ran over that morning and tore out several smoldering boards over the entryway. His actions kept the fire from spreading into the main part of the church building. I was able to clear away much of the damage by myself, and shortly after the raid we began to hold services.

The church also became a shelter for families who were now homeless. The entryway, the bullet holes in the woodwork, and the broken glass would all have to wait for repair until those staying in the church had rebuilt their homes and, most importantly, had begun rebuilding their lives.

***

Jordan was always on my mind. I wondered if his body was lying somewhere and would never be discovered. Or maybe the Confederates took him hostage because of his malevolent anti-slavery editorials in the paper, or the knowledge of the Underground Railroad they assumed he possessed.

The other mystery was an elder from my church—John Lykins. John had left town with his family a day or two before the horrible massacre, telling the other elders at church they were going to Missouri to visit relatives. It had been several days since the murderous attack on our city, and he and his family had not reappeared. I knew how slowly news traveled to rural areas, and my guess was that it simply took a while to reach him. I couldn't have been more wrong.

The mysterious disappearance of John Lykins began to unravel as I read a note written by a Lawrence clergyman, Reverend Hugh Fisher, given to one of his former parishioners before he left Kansas. The note ended up in the hands of a territorial marshal who came to me asking how well I knew Fisher and Lykins.

I had known Reverend Fisher as the pastor of the Methodist Episcopal Church in Lawrence, however, I and the other clergy had very little respect for him. We all knew that he smoked and drank, and there were also rumors that he skimmed money from the collection plate. These rumors were not difficult to believe given his crude and irreverent manner. Therefore, I read his claims concerning Quantrill's raid on Lawrence with some reservation. Yet even though he seemed predisposed as a thief and a liar, we were intrigued by his note which read:

> Spies were in town all night. Indeed it is placed beyond peradventure that the mother of a certain banker of Lawrence, who secured all his valuables the night before the raid, spent weeks with his family in Lawrence, and made a map of the town giving the names, residences, and location of those who were to be killed and their homes burned, marking them thus—"Kill and Burn," or "Burn," or if the property belonged to a sympathizer only "Kill." This map was taken by this heinous woman to Kansas City, and Quantrill and his lieutenants entertained day and night in the greatest possible seclusion in her parlor, where they had the maps explained preparatory to the sacking of Lawrence.

The note clearly portrayed John Lykins as a staunch Confederate and his mother as a spy for Quantrill and his raiders. I remember when his mother came to visit—John introduced me to her after church one Sunday. I couldn't believe it! Was it possible that one of my own elders was a spy and a murderer? If he was, then it meant that he marked my family to be killed. It was also possible he knew what happened to Jordan.

Colonel Eldridge and his regiment had been out almost a week chasing Quantrill and his bandits. On the morning of August 26th I was awakened by a loud pounding on my front door.

"Reverend Cole! Reverend Cole!"

I ran downstairs and answered the door. It was Wes Varner.

"What is it, Wes?"

"The colonel and his men are about a mile from Lawrence." The words tumbled out. "They've captured twelve of Quantrill's men and they're bringing them to town in chains!"

We mounted our horses and rode fast to town. An enormous crowd on Massachusetts Street stood waiting to see the men who murdered their families, and who also burned and ransacked the buildings along that very avenue. Their silence said it all. This was a moment we desired. This was an event we knew we had to witness. Yet, only a sorrowful anger permeated throughout the crowd.

The silence was broken as someone in the crowd shouted, "There they are!" We saw Colonel Eldridge on the lead horse with about forty other soldiers on horseback. Toward the end of the procession we saw a wagon with the captured men in chains walking behind it.

I don't know if I have ever seen a man who looked so tired and haggard. Eldridge was wearing his blue officer's uniform and an officer's hat with gold braid. Usually his uniform looked clean and bright. Today, however, his coat was dull from the dust and torn in several places, and his boots were muddy. It must have been quite a battle. As the colonel rode in, he took his hat off and wiped his forehead with a bandanna. Truly, he had gone a whole lot further than the extra mile for the citizens of Lawrence.

The crowd removed their hats as Colonel Eldridge and his men rode past, stopping in front of the jail where the colonel presented his prisoners to the town marshal. I was standing about thirty feet away from the prisoners who looked like a filthy ragamuffin band of villains. That's when I recognized one of the prisoners. It was John Lykins! Instantly I felt anger and rage. My neck felt hot under my collar, and my heart began to pound in my chest. I made a fist with both hands. For the first time in my life I felt as though I could kill a man with my bare hands.

"Joshua! I see him too. Leave him alone! Let them deal with him!" Wes shouted as I began running across the street.

Wes never called me Joshua—he always called me Reverend. I had the same respect for Wes as I did my own father, and I knew that at that moment he wasn't speaking to me as a minister, but as he would his own son. The colonel and his men only watched, but Wes grabbed me just as I reared back to hit Lykins.

"You'll regret it, son! He's not worth it!"

"What happened to my brother? Where's Jordan!" I shouted as I broke loose from Wes's grip. I grabbed Lykins by the collar while holding my fist up against his chin.

"I don't know," Lykins spoke in a low gruff voice through his clenched teeth. "I don't care about your Yankee brother. I hope he's dead!"

Wes grabbed me again and pulled me away—just as I spit hard directly in Lykin's face. At that particular moment I didn't care who saw me. I had never felt so betrayed in my life. A man who sat and discussed church, the Bible, worship—a man who pretended to be a leader in my congregation—had been part of a murderous rampage in our city. How could I forgive a man like that?

Thank God, justice was swift. The day of the hanging I sat on my front porch trying to get a handle on the hurt and pain in my heart. I later read about the execution in the *Leavenworth Daily Conservative*. The headline read: "Spy Hung in Lawrence," followed by these words:

> The "spy" confessed that he moved his
> family out of Lawrence the night prior to
> the raid and then rode in with Quantrill
> the next morning. After his confession, he
> was then hung.

Knowing Lykins was dead didn't heal my wounds. I felt more lost and alone than ever. That scared me. I knew I had suffered a great loss, but I also understood that I had much to look forward to (thinking of Elisabeth). The events of the past few weeks were tearing apart my future. I could not relate to Elisabeth and her love for the Lord in the state I was in. I had to get a hold on my emotions, and even more I needed a cleansing in my heart.

Reverend Morgan came for one of his monthly visits. My heart would leap for joy whenever I saw him riding toward the house. Every other month he would bring the entire family. Elisabeth and I wrote each other letters that her father would carry back and forth for us. Although I had not confided in Elisabeth concerning my inward struggles, I thanked God for her father's visits. He was the only one I felt comfortable sharing my spiritual battles with. I told him about my nightmares, my angry thoughts, and my feelings of guilt. I even shared with him how I spit in John Lykin's face and how I felt as though I could have killed him.

"I can't even pray, Mr. Morgan."

"That's serious, Joshua…that's very serious."

"I'm such a hypocrite! I preach on Sundays, and then come home and release all my anger on the chopping block, or by shouting as loudly as I can as I throw things in the house. I just can't seem to shake it off. I know that bitterness and fits of wrath are ungodly, but it makes me feel better—at least for the moment."

"Joshua, we know that one of the greatest apostles in the Bible fought spiritual battles just as we do. The apostle Paul said of himself in Romans 7:15 and 24, 'For what I am doing, I do not understand. For what I will to do, that I do not practice; but what I hate, that I do. O wretched man that I am! Who will deliver me from this body of death?' You're not alone, son. Many godly men have struggled with the same things."

"But what's the answer, Mr. Morgan?"

"You're doing one of the most important things right at this moment. You're asking for help."

When he said that, I began to cry. I felt like a little boy. After all, grown men don't cry—or so I thought.

"I'm sorry, Mr. Morgan," I said as I tried to choke back my tears, "I don't want you to think I'm a weakling or a coward."

Reverend Morgan lifted my chin and looked me in the eyes. "Joshua, listen to me. Don't think for one moment I believe you're weak. I admire you for the way you've stood up and handled this tragedy in your life. Truthfully, I would be concerned about you if you didn't break down and cry once in a while. I would think you didn't have a heart. Showing your emotions doesn't make you less of a man. Being a man has to do with standing up when duty calls, showing courage in the face of trials and tribulation, and living a life of integrity and honor before God and before men. You've exhibited all those characteristics. Besides that, a real man has a compassionate heart that can be touched by God and knows how to call out to Him. He knows how to be compassionate and courageous at the same time."

"But how do I deal with this anger? I know exactly what Paul felt like—a wretched man."

"A lot of scriptures come to mind," Reverend Morgan said as he opened his Bible. "After the apostle Paul wrote about feeling like a wretched man, he went on to say in Romans 8:1-2: 'There is therefore now no condemnation to them which are in Christ Jesus, who walk not after the flesh, but after the Spirit. For the law of the Spirit of life in Christ Jesus hath made me free from the law of sin and death.'

He closed his bible. "You're feeling condemned because you're giving in to the flesh—doing things that make you feel good for the moment, but don't bring peace to your soul. Condemnation comes from the devil, and it stares at us when we live our lives according to the flesh. We become free from condemnation through Christ when we walk according to His Spirit. In other words, we become free when we rely completely upon His strength and power and not our own strength."

"But how do we do that?"

"Could the slaves your family helped become free by themselves? If they could, then why did they need your help? Even if they could get to the North without help, are they truly free unless someone declares them to be? It takes humility to seek and receive help. That's what you're doing today. The apostle Paul also taught that we become slaves to whomever we present ourselves—if we present ourselves to sin, we become slaves of sin. If we present ourselves to the Lord and His Spirit, we become slaves of righteousness. The Lord has declared us to be free if we have accepted Him as our Savior. Joshua, according to God's Word you're free. But you have to present yourself to the Lord on a daily basis through prayer, worship, and study of His Word."

"That, Mr. Morgan, is where I'm having the difficulty."

"Joshua, you're making it more difficult than it really is. Whether you realize it or not, you've already demonstrated to me that your heart is tender toward the Lord. You just need to understand how the Word of God relates to your situation. Faith comes by hearing. But, more importantly, faith without works is dead. As necessary as it is to discuss God's Word and how it relates to our lives, if we don't act upon what we know is truth, we're deceiving ourselves. Our faith will not be effective. Let's pray together that you can begin to act upon God's Word."

I bowed my head and waited for Reverend Morgan to pray.

"Joshua...I want you to pray."

"I'm sorry, Mr. Morgan, but I can't."

"You mean you *won't*."

He wasn't harsh with me, but he was stern like Father used to be. I knew I was between a rock and hard place. Reverend Morgan had spoken well of me and been more than encouraging. The graciousness his family showed me was beyond anything I had ever experienced. He even trusted me to get to know his daughter—not to mention the fact that I was also a minister. I had great respect for him as a man of God, but I couldn't pray just to appease him, or because I owed him something. He would see through that in a heartbeat. It had to be genuine.

"I'm sorry, sir, but I'm not sure that I can."

"Well, I can't make you pray, and God certainly won't. The fact is, we do what we want to do. Your desire is gone. But it can be restored. Joshua, I'm going to read a passage to you out of the 51st Psalm. I want you to pay attention, and afterward what I have read is exactly what we're going to pray—together."

As Reverend Morgan began to read, my heart began to soften. Listening to the words of the psalm, I knew it was what I desired.

"Okay Joshua, now we're going to pray that psalm together just as if we're praying for ourselves. I can't make it come from your heart, but I hope that it does. Pray this after me, son: 'Father, purge me with hyssop, and I shall be clean: Lord wash me, and I shall be whiter than snow. I ask you, Lord, to cause me to hear joy and gladness; that the bones which thou has broken may rejoice. Please Lord, hide thy face from my sins, and blot out all mine iniquities. Create in me a clean heart, O God; and renew a right spirit within me. Cast me not away from thy presence; and take not thy Holy Spirit from me.' In Jesus' name I pray, amen."

After praying those words, I felt a warmth in my heart that hadn't been there for several months. I knew we had broken through a barrier. Tears ran down my face as we stood.

Reverend Morgan gave me a fatherly embrace, then he told me he wanted to stay and help me catch up on some chores. That afternoon we chopped wood, shoveled manure, and repaired several things around the house that were still damaged from the raid. In the evening we sat on the porch and visited until sunset. This was the most peaceful I had been since the massacre. One thing still bothered me, however, which I shared with my friend.

"I haven't been able to get my mind settled concerning the sovereignty of God. According to what I've been taught, my family was predestined to die last August. But that would also mean God used evil men to murder them. To me, that doesn't square with the truth according to the apostle John that God is love."

"You sure are a thinker, Joshua—I like that. We cannot deny the fact that God is sovereign. If He wasn't sovereign, He wouldn't be God. We also know that within His sovereignty He has given mankind freewill, meaning freedom to make our own choices whether for good or evil. That truth is evident from the very beginning when Adam and Eve sinned against the Lord.

"Be that as it may, the truth concerning man's freewill does not demean the sovereignty of God; it actually magnifies or exalts His sovereignty because only an all-powerful God could create mankind in such a way. It also proves the love of God in that He would allow us to love Him of our own freewill and not because He forces us too.

"Along with all of this truth is also the truth that mankind in his carnality can choose evil instead of good. And, unfortunately, when mankind chooses evil, those who have chosen good will be affected sooner or later. But for those who have chosen the Lord and His commandments, His unwavering love will pick us back up, dust off the trials and tribulations, and set us back on the path of love and righteousness. We also believe that in the end He will judge the living and the dead, good and evil, for all eternity. He alone will cast the final judgment on every soul for the works they have done in their bodies."

I stared at Reverend Morgan, not saying a word as I allowed what he said to sink in. As it did, tears of joy began running down my face. He had explained in less than six minutes what all of my college professors couldn't explain in six years!

"Joshua, are you okay?"

"So God didn't take my family, Mr. Morgan?"

"No, son...evil men killed your family. Not only is your family in heaven where you will see them again one day, but the Lord loves you very much. He will not only help you get back on your feet but, according to the Bible, it's His desire to give you a future and a hope."

We sat and talked a while longer before it was time for Reverend Morgan to leave. As he mounted his horse and rode off, I knew that I wasn't alone anymore. My earthly father was gone, but I still had the Lord. He had proven his love for me by providing a mentor—a man who loved and cared for me just as my own father had done. In the days to come, this relationship would continue to grow stronger. And I also would continue to discover how little I knew about the Lord, and just how much I needed to trust in Him and have faith in His Word.

To the Stars Through Difficulties

A statement from one of the survivors of the massacre helped our community focus once again on the underlying reasons we had settled in Kansas. Hannah Oliver was quoted as saying, "The motives for the settling of Kansas were social and moral, and the issues were stupendous."

These words were used as a catalyst to rally Lawrence to rise from the ashes. The townspeople adopted the slogan: "From Ashes to Immortality," while the state of Kansas used as its motto: "Ad Astra per Aspera"—To the Stars Through Difficulties. We had experienced more than our share of difficulties, but by God's grace we were able to rise to the challenge.

Within days after the raid, money and supplies poured into Lawrence from all over the territory and from the East. Two companies of Union troops were also sent to Lawrence to secure the city while its citizens rebuilt. The troops ended up staying until the war was over.

The presence of these troops allowed Colonel Eldridge and his brother to begin rebuilding their hotel. Considering all the run-ins the colonel had with bands of pro-slavery bandits, Quantrill and his murderers surely took pleasure in burning the Eldridge House just as the infamous sheriff Sam Jones and his pro-slavery bandits did in 1856. Originally their hotel was called the Free State Hotel, and like so many things in Lawrence helped make clear our intention to see Kansas enter the Union as a Free State.

The Free State Hotel was also a place where many settlers stayed while building their homes in Lawrence. Like all of the other destruction to the city, the burning of the hotel was deliberate and decisive. But the colonel and his brother were stubborn. After capturing over forty of Quantrill's raiders, and after he saw to it that Union troops would help secure the city, he spoke at a city meeting. In his speech he vowed that he would not be defeated, and that the Eldridges would build their hotel bigger and better. Their boldness gave courage and resolve to the rest of Lawrence's citizens.

Throughout the fall and winter of 1863, and into the spring of 1864, we put our hands to the work of reconstruction with great diligence. I watched and listened to the people around me as a remarkable transformation took place, amazed by their resilience and stamina. As the community worked together tearing down old buildings, burning huge piles of refuse, and putting up new structures, I was reminded of the early settlement days. There is a wonderful camaraderie ignited in working together for a common cause. We knew we could count on each other. The work strengthened families and friendships. It also helped mask many of the horrible memories of the recent past.

As a fresh wind blew upon Lawrence, we had renewed hope for the future. A little less than one year later, little evidence of Quantrill's raid would remain, and the people of Lawrence seemed to have even more zeal to help runaway slaves. We would survive. We would move on. But most importantly, we would always remember how the Lord enabled us to rise from the ashes.

A confidence was even building within us that the war couldn't last much longer. President Lincoln had appointed Ulysses S. Grant as the general-in-chief of the Union Army, and the people in the North expected him to bring quick and decisive victory. It would still take nearly a year, and there were many battles yet to be fought, but we believed our righteous cause would prevail.

Though Kansas contributed scores of men during the war, and was home to numerous skirmishes with Confederate guerillas, Mine Creek was the sight of the only major Civil War battle fought in our state. The papers reported that the battle involved some 25,000 men. The Union Army under Generals Curtis, Blunt, and Pleasanton defeated the Confederate Army under Generals Price and Marmaduke. In hindsight this battle would prove to end the Confederate threat in Kansas.

In celebration and praise to God for the victory He had given our troops, our congregation adopted a fresh new hymn, written in 1862 by Julia Ward Howe. We discovered the hymn after the words were reprinted in one of our local newspapers and it became a favorite amongst my parishioners.

Mine eyes have seen the glory of
the coming of the Lord.

He is trampling out the vintage
where the grapes of wrath are stored;

He hath loosed the fateful lightning
of His terrible, swift sword.

His truth is marching on.

I have seen Him in the watch fires of
a hundred circling camps;

They have builded Him an altar in
the evening dews and damps;

I can read His righteous sentence by
the dim and flaring lamps.

His day is marching on.

I have read a fiery gospel writ in
burnished rows of steel;

As ye deal with my contemnors, so
with you my grace shall deal;

Let the Hero, born of woman, crush
the serpent with his heal.

Since God is marching on.

In the beauty of the lilies Christ was
born across the sea,

With a glory in his bosom that
transfigures you and me.

As He died to make men holy, let us
die to make men free,

While God is marching on.

I watched as my congregation sang this hymn with
tears glistening in their eyes. Their faces spoke of firsthand knowledge of the ravages of war as almost everyone
had lost loved ones during the massacre, and also within

the war itself. They had a deep appreciation for all who had died while advancing the cause of freedom. Many of my parishioners spoke of how Julia Ward Howe had penned some of their deepest feelings.

As only the Lord can, He used many different avenues and many different voices to help put Lawrence back on its feet. Our church came alive again. The community was springing to life as well, and the war news appeared to be in our favor. I saw smiles on people's faces. I saw hope in their eyes. I heard laughter in the stores and on the streets. For the first time I was confident that we would not only move on, but we would become strong again. One of the avenues that the Lord used to bless my life and to show me His love, however, would take me completely by surprise.

The city of Lawrence was not only rebuilding at an incredible pace, it was actually growing in population. When word got out that Union troops were stationed in town, we had an influx of new residents. I began working part-time for Wes Varner as his lumber and hardware business was booming. I could not only make some extra money, but could also help bring in needed supplies for new buildings and homes.

One evening, after a long day of hauling lumber and building supplies from the ferryboat to downtown Lawrence, I headed home to my big empty house. As I turned the wagon onto Somerset Lane I saw several people sitting on the ground in front of my house. I was halfway down the lane when it dawned on me who they were.

It was the Higgins family—the homesteaders I had met shortly after my return to Lawrence.

"Howdy, Reverend."

"Jake, Sue Ellen, kids—it sure is good to see you. What brings you up to Lawrence?"

"Well sir, we heard about the shootin' and killin', and we figured we'd come and lend a hand."

Jake and Sue Ellen had hearts as big as all outdoors. However, their timing was a little off—by about seven or eight months. I wasn't quite sure what to tell them.

"Well Jake, I'm sure the folks here appreciate your thoughtfulness and generosity, but the city seems to be getting back on its feet. I'm not sure there's much to do."

"We don't mean to offend," Sue Ellen spoke up, "but we're not here for the city folk, Reverend. We're here for you. We heard you lost your kin, and we've been hurtin' for you. We just thought we'd do some cookin' and cleanin'—really anythin' to be a blessin' to you."

I was speechless. A family that had next to nothing, folks who needed more help than what they even understood, wanted to do something for *me*. If I let my pride get in the way I would offend them, and I wouldn't do that for all the wealth in the world.

"Oh it's not that, Sue Ellen. You're welcome to stay as long as you like. I've got plenty of room, and I sure would enjoy the company. But it's just me here in the house, and I'm not sure what you would have to do. I don't want you to feel like you made this trip for nothing."

"There's always somethin' to be done," Jake said, as he began to walk the team and the wagon back to the barn. "I promise we won't be burdensome, Reverend. If we can be a blessin', then it won't be for nothin'."

For the next two weeks Jake and Sue Ellen wouldn't allow me to lift a finger. Sue Ellen turned out to be a decent cook when given the proper tools to work with. (Of course, just about anyone's cooking was better than mine.) Jake cleaned the barn, checked the horse's shoes, cut the brush by the woods, scythed the tall grass in the lane, shoveled manure, and plowed the garden for spring planting. I've seen very few couples work so hard with such big smiles on their faces. They were dirt-poor settlers, but they were probably two of the happiest and hardest working people I knew.

My only frustration with Jake and Sue Ellen was getting them to allow me to bless them. They would not take anything without trying to give something in return. I tried to give Jake some money one day, and I'll never forget what he said: "Reverend, with all due respect, I don't want any reward from you. I want my reward to come from God. Besides, my daddy told me to always give more than I've taken."

In the evenings we sat on the front porch and they asked question after question about the Bible. The two children, Rance and Charlotte, were very well-behaved. They played quietly on the porch until sunset, while I taught the Bible to their parents. It was during one of those times in the evening that the great amount of respect I already had for Jake increased even more.

"Reverend, I just can't get enough Bible teaching."

"Jake, would you please call me 'Joshua'? For heaven's sake, you're living in my house."

"No, sir. You're a man of God, and it's only fittin' that I show proper respect." Sue Ellen nodded her head in agreement.

"Okay, I won't argue with you about that. But there is one thing that I really want you and Sue Ellen to do."

"Yes sir, what might that be?"

"Would you and your family please sleep on the beds instead of the floor? And you don't have to all stay in one room, Jake. There are four other bedrooms; you could at least use two."

"Thank you much, Reverend, but we'd feel too funny stayin' in beds that belonged to your dead loved ones. I'd feel like I'm disgracin' 'em all."

There was no convincing them. I disagreed with Jake's reasoning, but I sure respected the way he loved and honored others. They continued to sleep on the floor in one bedroom, they ate very little food, and they worked like they were laborers on a plantation. I felt guilty knowing that while I was out during the day, the Higgins family was busy cooking, cleaning, and working at my house. I learned so much from this poor pioneering family. I learned what true respect and honor looked and sounded like. I saw genuine self-sacrifice firsthand. I was eyewitness to the greatest lesson of all— to love your neighbor as yourself. After two weeks, they felt that it was time to leave.

"Reverend Cole, we sure thank you for your kindness."

"*My* kindness, Jake? I could never repay you for all you've done!"

"No need, Reverend, but we're gonna have to be leavin' in the mornin'."

"Jake, I know you don't want anything in return for how you've blessed my life, but I'm going to give you and your family a few things whether you like it or not. You can take them with you tomorrow, or I can bring to your place and drop them off. Either way, I insist that you take what I give."

"But, Reverend…"

"Jake, if you respect me as a man of God, I want you to give me your word that whatever I choose to send with you, you will take without argument."

"You put me in a hard place."

"Yes I have, but it's for your own good. God wants to bless you, and you have to be able to receive God's blessings the same as you give to others."

"Reverend, I do respect you, so I give you my word."

This was going to be fun! I hadn't been this happy since I went to see Elisabeth last summer. Our family had been so blessed with so many things—food, clothes, tools, livestock. I had given away a lot my family's clothes to those who were homeless after the massacre. Though I would keep all of Jordan's things in hopes that he would return, I still had quite a few of my father and mother's clothes I could give away. Mother was a fantastic seamstress. She made her own dresses as well as clothes for the rest of the family.

When the Higgins family showed up at my house, they had the clothes on their backs and one horse. That means they took turns walking and riding for ten miles in order to get to Lawrence. We had two wagons. I kept the smaller one in the barn which I knew Jake and Sue Ellen could certainly use. We also had an abundance of pistols and rifles in the house, and I knew Jake did a lot of hunting to provide food for his family. I couldn't wait to see their faces when I loaded a wagon for them. And I was counting on the fact that Jake had given me his word.

Before sunup, I went out to the barn and the fun began. I took one of our six horses, harnessed it next to Jake's, and then rigged them to our small wagon. I loaded my college trunk with six dresses, four pairs of men's pants, several nightshirts, and some extra dress material that mother had stored, along with a box of sewing items and buttons. I put the trunk in the rear of the wagon with a burlap sack containing a sack of flour, a sack of sugar, and several jars of preserves. Then I wrapped two rifles, two pistols, and a small box of ammunition in a blanket, tied a rope around it, and put in on the floorboard of the wagon; added a couple handsaws, a hammer, and a box of nails, an axe, and a jar of wagon grease, and I was done. I tied one of our plow mules behind the wagon, and then took the wagon around to the front of the house. After preparing the wagon, I made breakfast for everyone.

"Thank you again, Reverend, for allowin' us to stay in your fine home, and for the fine breakfast. We'd better be leavin' now. I'll fetch the horse from the barn."

"Hang on, Jake. I already brought your horse around front."

"That's kind of you sir," Jake said, as he began leading his family toward the front door.

"Jake, before you step outside, I want to remind you of the promise you made."

"Yes sir, I remember and I'll be grateful to you."

I almost couldn't contain my excitement as Jake, Sue Ellen, and the kids stepped out on the front porch. There was silence as they stared at the wagon with the trunk and sacks in the rear, puzzled looks on their faces. Then Jake spoke up, "Reverend, you got our horse fixed to your wagon."

"That's not my wagon, Jake. The horses, the mule, the wagon, and everything in it are yours."

"Jake, we can't take all that!"

"Hush up, Sue Ellen! I gave Reverend Cole my word that whatever he had for us this mornin' we would accept and be grateful for."

Sue Ellen began to cry as she walked over to the wagon and looked at its contents. "No one has ever cared for us this way, Reverend."

"I could say the same thing, Sue Ellen."

"We're grateful for all you've done, Reverend, and we'll never forget this." Jake looked me square in the eyes and shook my hand.

Sue Ellen and the children gave me a hug, then they all climbed up in the wagon—Sue Ellen in front with Jake, and Rance and Charlotte in the back. The little ones had big smiles on their faces as Jake snapped the reins and the wagon began to bounce down the lane.

It is truly more blessed to give. I was sad that they were leaving, but in my heart I had joy knowing I had been able to help them. The truth is the Higgins family helped me more than they could ever know. They taught me about God's love, and about sacrificial giving, and they helped fill a hole in my heart I thought was destined to remain empty.

"Are you taking in any passengers?" Wes asked as he continued to tear out fire damage.

Wes and I were finally repairing the porch over the entrance to the church. The bullet holes in the walls were not difficult to plug; however, each time we thought we were finished, we discovered one more. Our new windows had arrived, and two new doors. There was also quite a bit of minor damage to the interior woodwork that needed attention. Now that the city and its citizens seemed to be getting on with their lives, we had more time to devote to repairing the church.

"I'd love to take in passengers, Wes, but it's not possible right now. Being in the house alone, there's just no way for me to ensure their safety. I've been helping the Killions with receiving passengers and gathering supplies. Their house isn't far from the river, so it's become the last stop before the runaways leave town."

"That's good. You've got to stay involved. Now, let me ask you another question. You're twenty-six years old, Reverend Cole. What about marriage?"

I turned and gave Wes a surprised look and a sheepish grin. The question seemed to come out of nowhere, but I was glad he asked. I needed a little encouragement.

"Well, I've thought a lot about marriage lately. It's a desire of mine to get married someday and have a family."

"Do you have anyone in mind, Reverend?"

Seeing the smile on my face, Wes said, "I guess there's no need for you to answer that question. Is it someone from Lawrence? Anyone I know?"

"She's from Topeka, and her father is a Free Methodist minister."

"Well, what's her name, son? Don't keep me guessing."

"Her name is Elisabeth Morgan. She's beautiful, Wes! She's intelligent, she's gracious, and boy, does she love the Lord. Her family is wonderful too. They're very down to earth, and they have a deep commitment to God. They were there for me when I was grieving. They even helped me bury my family. I have the same respect for Reverend Morgan that I do for you and my own father. He has really gone out of his way to help me through a very difficult time."

"When do we get to meet them?"

"Well, Elisabeth and I are not officially courting. We've written a lot of letters to each other, and I see her and her family every other month. Even so, we haven't had any conversations about courtship. I hope that will change real soon."

I asked Wes to keep our conversation quiet, and I knew he would. He was a trustworthy man. Our conversation did increase my desire to begin moving in the direction of courtship and marriage, however. I knew in my heart that Elisabeth was a woman I could raise a family with, and spend the rest of my life with. I just wasn't sure how she felt. I was anxious to find out.

I had not been able to spend much time in Topeka, so I was glad the Morgans continued to visit me on a regular basis. Unfortunately, I had never developed any cooking skills. At Yale, Harry and I usually ate in the dining hall with the other divinity students. At home, the fire pit belonged to Father while the kitchen belonged to Mother. When it came to the kitchen, she didn't allow the men to pretend to know what they were doing.

Thank goodness Elisabeth and her mother always volunteered to cook whenever the family visited. I would object, but not very convincingly. I was thrilled to have a well-cooked meal in my own house. I was sure that Elisabeth and her mother would also rather eat something they'd cooked.

"I'm sorry I don't have many supplies. I've been fortunate to have a lot of church folks invite me over for supper this past year."

"Joshua, I really don't mind," Mrs. Morgan said as she put an apron on and began getting out pots and pans. "Elisabeth and I will cook something, and it will be wonderful. Don't worry."

⌐

"You ladies never cease to amaze me! It's hard to believe you made such a fine meal out of the paltry amount of food I have in the pantry."

"Actually Joshua, you have more in the pantry than you think," Mrs. Morgan said. "But we did take the liberty of throwing a few things out that were spoiled. I hope you don't mind."

"I'm sure it was necessary." I laughed. "As you can tell I'm not much of a homemaker." Then I asked, "Reverend and Mrs. Morgan, would you mind if Elisabeth and I took a little walk? We won't go far from the house."

"We don't mind, Joshua." Reverend Morgan replied. "When you come back we'll have some coffee on the stove. Then we can all visit."

It was nice to have a few moments alone with Elisabeth. We'd had very few opportunities to talk by ourselves since the day we picnicked together in Topeka, the day my family was murdered.

"It seems as though our getting to know one another—which I thought began beautifully—was cut short. I'm sorry about that."

"It's certainly understandable, Joshua, and yes, I thought it began very nicely too. How are you doing—spiritually I mean."

"I suppose your father has told you about some of our conversations."

"No, he hasn't. Whenever anyone confides in Father he holds it in confidence. I could sense he was bothered a few times after returning from his visits, but I didn't know what it was all about."

I already admired Revered Morgan. He had become a mentor and surrogate father to me. And after Elisabeth told me that he didn't tell her what I had been going through, I admired him even more—if that were possible. He was a man I could trust, and men such as that are difficult to find. When you do, they're worth more than gold. It was better that I discuss my struggles with Elisabeth face-to-face, though I was concerned how she might react.

"Elisabeth, there's some things I must tell you. The events last August really shook my faith. I was mad at God, I was mad at people, and I was filled with rage. I became so full of anger that I couldn't even pray. I felt hatred in my heart and, worse yet, I felt like the world's worst hypocrite."

Elisabeth listened with great interest as I continued to tell her about my spiritual trials and spiritual renewal. I told her all about being betrayed by an elder in my church, and how I spit in his face. I told her how I wanted to see him hang, but then after he was dead I still wasn't satisfied. I confided in her about my nightmares and the guilt I felt over not being there for my family. I even confessed to her that at one point I wished I had died with them.

I didn't realize how long I had talked until we heard her father call from the porch that the coffee was ready. On the way back to the house I explained to her how the Lord dealt with my hurt and pain and how thankful I was for her father and his tenacity, compassion, and wisdom. I then assured Elisabeth that now I was okay, and was spending time with the Lord once again.

She simply smiled and said, "That's good, I'm glad to hear that."

I wasn't sure how Elisabeth felt about everything I told her. However, I was glad I had confided in her.

As we sat down to have coffee, Reverend Morgan asked about the city and the reconstruction efforts.

"So Joshua, fill us in on how things are going in the city. I haven't had the opportunity to take a close look, but from the little I've seen it seems the rebuilding process is going very well."

"Truthfully, it's amazing how far we've come," I replied. "Seven months ago, I would've never imagined we'd be so far along. I sense a hope, a joy, and an expectation I wasn't sure I'd ever see again. Only the Lord can rebuild lives and bring such new beginnings."

"I believe you're right," said Mrs. Morgan.

"What about your family newspaper, Joshua. Are you going to start it up again?" Reverend Morgan asked.

"No. I've had several offers on the building and the equipment. Right now the *Kansas State Journal* is using our offices to print. Since our newspaper office was the only one not completely destroyed after the raid, I let them begin publishing almost immediately. They've done a great job keeping up with current events, and I've been impressed with how they've used the paper to help rally folks to rebuild. Anyway, the newspaper had really become Raymond and Jordan's business. I'm considering selling everything to the *Journal*. They would like that because they're already at home in the offices. My heart's desire is to focus on ministry, home, and family. The money I would gain through selling the business would go a long way toward starting a family."

"That's what we really wanted to know, Joshua." Mrs. Morgan laughed a little.

I was puzzled. Elisabeth's mother and father were both smiling, and Elisabeth was blushing.

Mrs. Morgan continued. "What we are wondering about is whether or not you and Elisabeth are considering courting one another? Please understand we're not trying to push you. We know that you've been through a lot. And we certainly don't want to suggest anything that both of you are not comfortable with."

"Oh, I'm sorry for being so slow in understanding," I said somewhat embarrassed. "We haven't had much time to talk about courtship. Despite everything that's happened, however, the idea of courtship has entered my mind."

There was a long pause. Finally Elisabeth spoke up. "Can we take it slowly? I feel we're rushing things."

Almost immediately I spoke up and said, "I agree."

I was concerned. Truthfully I didn't agree with Elisabeth. I only agreed with her because of my pride. I felt like I was being brushed aside, and I didn't like it. There didn't seem to be any enthusiasm about courtship in Elisabeth's voice, and more importantly the glimmer was gone from her eyes. Something had changed. I wondered if it had to do with what I had confided to her during our walk. I didn't want to ask in front of her parents, so the answer would have to wait.

Unequally Yoked?

*S*everal weeks passed since the awkward moment of being presented with the suggestion of courtship by Elisabeth's parents, and then feeling as though I was being brushed aside. I completely understood how the idea of courtship would make Elisabeth nervous; it made me nervous too. Nonetheless, I was at least willing to talk about it.

As the Morgans arrived one afternoon for another visit, I was hoping the awkwardness had passed. Yet I could tell Elisabeth had something on her mind. I assumed it was the same thing I had on my mind. I was anxious to find out. After supper that evening, her parents stayed on the porch as Elisabeth and I sat on the bench at the end of the lane.

The awkwardness had certainly passed, and the time had come for us to speak openly and honestly about the subject of courtship. It began pleasantly enough. We reminisced about our letters and our conversations and how, within them, we had both expressed great joy over our friendship, and how deeply we cared for each other. We had never mentioned the word love, but it always seemed to be on the tips of our tongues—or the tips of our pens as it were. We also both agreed that there was no reason for courtship unless marriage was in our future. Therefore, for us to speak of courtship also meant we were heading toward marriage.

After we had expressed our feelings, and discussed the past and present, we began speaking of the future. That's when Elisabeth's true concern surfaced, and I wasn't pleased with the direction the conversation went.

"I don't understand, Elisabeth. You're telling me that we shouldn't court each other because I don't speak in other tongues?"

"Joshua, it goes much deeper than that."

I was tired of hearing about the baptism of the Holy Spirit, and speaking in other tongues. I kept hoping this discussion would simply disappear. To me it was inconceivable that a woman could love a man, but choose not to marry him due to a theological difference of opinions. As far as I was concerned, the commitment to love, honor, protect, and provide for a wife should never hinge upon whether or not I spoke in other tongues. As the discussion unfolded, it reminded me of my first encounter with Elisabeth. I hated disagreeing with her.

Our conversation also reminded me of the discussions I used to have with Harry. The only times we seemed to argue was when we discussed the spiritual gifts, although Harry and I could argue vehemently with each other and still remain close friends. Maybe I expected the same thing with Elisabeth, and yet it wasn't the same. The difference with Elisabeth was the possibility of courtship and marriage. I was so aggravated that this doctrine had resurfaced at one of the most important junctures in my life.

Father's advice sprang up in my mind: Discuss these matters before marriage, and don't discover such a disagreement afterward. But was this doctrine worth arguing over? I had never considered the possibility of a man and woman disavowing courtship because of a disagreement over the spiritual gifts. As far as I was concerned, it was all based on emotion and it wasn't necessary for Christians today.

I could feel my face turning red as I said, "It seems as though you're questioning the depth of my relationship with the Lord."

"Joshua, I'm not questioning whether or not you're born again, or if you love the Lord. And I believe if we were to marry, we would both be committed to the marriage. But being in agreement with my future husband concerning the Holy Spirit is very important to me. In Amos it says, 'How can two walk together unless they agree?'"

"How often do couples getting married agree on every little portion of Scripture?"

"That's not what I'm expecting, Joshua. Once we're married, Christ calls me to submit to my husband. However, that means I have to be settled in my heart before I enter into courtship with anyone. There are minor biblical issues we can agree to disagree on, but I do believe it's very important for us to be in agreement on major doctrines. You may not consider the baptism of the Holy Spirit a major doctrine, but it is to me.

"I'm trusting in the Lord for a man who is a spiritual leader," she continued, "someone who will lead his family in these important truths. I believe it's God's desire that my future husband and I raise our children in the Holy Spirit and power. I'm not trying to sound holier-than-thou, but I have a deep appreciation for the difference it makes in the life of a believer. I've experienced the powerful way God leads and uses those who are baptized in His Spirit, and in my heart I know it would always be a bone of contention between us."

"But Elisabeth, how can you be so sure about this doctrine? Isn't it just your interpretation based on your feelings?"

"Election and predestination are based on interpretation. There are points concerning those doctrines we see eye to eye on, and some we don't. As far as I'm concerned, that's okay because Scripture is not as clear on those subjects. But Joshua, when it comes to the baptism of the Holy Spirit, I haven't given you my interpretation of Scripture. I've recited what Scripture plainly says, and I believe it. Furthermore, I not only believe it, I've experienced it."

"How do you know that people who speak in tongues today are experiencing the same thing that occurred on the Day of Pentecost? What if you're wrong, Elisabeth?"

"How do you know when someone is speaking French? How do you know English is truly English? My grandmother told me that her grandmother heard people speak in tongues during the Edwards' revivals in the East. That was over one hundred years ago. You know as well as I do that during the Cane Ridge revivals in Kentucky in the 1820s, Presbyterians and Methodists together experienced the power of God. It's been recorded that many people fell under the power of God, and folks prophesied and spoke in tongues.

"Christians have been speaking in other tongues since the Holy Spirit was poured out, and they have recognized what it sounds like and its powerful impact ever since. You told me that the first time you heard anyone speak in tongues was your college roommate. How did you know he was speaking in tongues if you had only read about it but never heard it?"

"It still doesn't make sense, Elisabeth. You believe that God is powerful enough to do these fanatical things, and I believe God is powerful enough He doesn't have to use those fanatical things. Most importantly, if speaking in tongues is not scriptural, and if it is not God's will for us today, then you're telling me you're willing to throw away a future together based upon a doctrine of fanaticism!"

"No, Joshua. What I'm saying is that I believe the Lord will bring a man into my life who desires everything the Lord has for him; a man who takes God at His word, and is not afraid of what others think of him. A man who is willing to accept everything the Lord offers by faith—including the things that seem foolish—even if those who consider themselves wise condemn him for it. I am truly concerned about you, Joshua! You are so afraid that you might become radical, or you might look foolish in the eyes of men. Yet God has said He uses foolish things to confound the wise. You're being confounded and you don't even know it.

"Tell me how Jesus spoke the worlds into existence," She was stirred up now. "Tell me how Jesus was born of a virgin after the Holy Spirit overshadowed Mary. You believe those doctrinal truths, and yet you can't figure them out with your mind. On the other hand, you will question the supernatural validity of the baptism of the Holy Spirit because if you accept it, it might cause you to look silly.

"You have a brilliant mind, Joshua. My concern for you is that too often you allow your mind to rule over your heart. True belief—faith—comes from the heart. You asked how we know if someone who speaks in tongues is a true believer. We know the same way Jesus knew that the Pharisees were charlatans—by their fruit. Do you honestly think I'm possessed or being used by the devil?"

I had never seen Elisabeth this passionate. She wasn't angry or hateful. Rather, there was a sorrowful sound to her voice, and the look on her face was the look of a person who had summoned emotions from the deepest part of their being. Tears began to roll down her cheeks as she stared at me with a questioning look on her face. I don't know why, but I couldn't answer her. I couldn't even form any words. At that moment, all of my theological training was useless. Do I answer her question from my head, or from my heart? I wondered. *Was she being deceived by the devil? I would lose her if I said yes. But if I said no I would be admitting to something I still wasn't convinced of.* I didn't like the feeling of being pushed into a corner, so I sat silent.

Through her tears Elisabeth said, "You've answered my question without saying a word. You've also brought to light the deeper issue, Joshua. I have shared my heart with you, and you still don't know me! I won't marry a man who thinks I'm foolish for what I believe, or who thinks I simply give in to fits of emotions and fanaticism."

At that moment pride took over. My heart wanted to cry out for help and a deeper relationship with God, but my body would not allow it. Arrogant and foolhardy, I sat silent as Elisabeth walked away. Suddenly I was alone on the bench under the majestic elms on Somerset Lane. It was a beautiful evening, I was sitting in my favorite spot on God's green earth, a place where I had learned the Bible, yet at that moment I felt as though I knew nothing. Even worse, the woman I desired to marry was walking away with my heart in her hands.

Elisabeth walked directly to the family's buggy and climbed up in the seat. Her parents knew what that meant. Reverend Morgan gave Mrs. Morgan a hand up into the buggy, and then he walked over to me, put his hand on my shoulder, and said, "I'll be back soon, and we'll talk."

My heart sank as the Morgan's black buggy disappeared on the horizon. What bothered me the most was that Elisabeth had read me like a book. If this were a game of chess, she just placed me in checkmate. But this wasn't a game of chess; it was our future.

I believed in God, and I took pride in having knowledge of the Bible, but I was afraid of showing any emotion. As ridiculous as it sounds, I feared a deeper relationship with the Lord through the baptism of the Holy Spirit because of the way it might cause me to speak or act. All these years my intellect had protected my heart from hurt and pain, and it had shielded me from looking "foolish." I kept my heart in a box and responded to life's trials with what I called a "rational thought process." What I failed to realize was how part of that process involved locking up my heart so tightly that even the truest love couldn't pry it open.

Even though Elisabeth didn't fully recognize it, I had opened my heart and let her in. Then, without me realizing it, the Lord used her to expose what was hidden in the dark corners. And now my ugly pride was causing me to break two hearts at once, just when mine seemed to be healing. That moment was not only etched in my mind, but it was also engraved on a sorrowful and broken heart. This time, however, I was determined not to allow it to become hard.

—

I stewed about our conversation for the next three weeks. One moment I was filled with sadness, and the next puffed up with arrogance. Elisabeth had not only challenged my doctrine, she had also challenged my pride. As the days passed by, the part of me that missed her, and daydreamed about our future together, began to soften my heart. I longed to see her again.

After a month and a half I became concerned that the entire Morgan family didn't want to have anything to do with me. Elisabeth's words continually rolled through my mind. Even though my pride didn't want to agree with her, my intellect couldn't prove her wrong. I still wasn't ready to wholeheartedly accept the baptism of the Holy Spirit, but I did desire more discussion on the subject. After two months, that seemed like an eternity, I saw Reverend Morgan riding toward the house.

"But Reverend Morgan," I said as we sat and visited on the front porch, "how is she not questioning my sincerity before the Lord? For that matter, even whether or not I'm born again?"

"That's your pride talking, Joshua. Listen, if I have four horses hitched to a plow and you have two horses hitched to a plow, and we're both plowing a field, does that mean the one who has four horses is a real farmer and the other isn't? Elisabeth isn't judging whether or not you're born again, or whether or not you love the Lord. We simply believe that there is more the Lord has for us after the born-again experience. Let me ask you something: Did the disciples receive the Holy Spirit in the upper room when Jesus breathed on them?"

"I'd have to say yes. After all, Jesus did say, 'receive the Holy Spirit'."

"Okay. Now let me ask you another question. If they received the Holy Spirit in John chapter twenty—the same day as the resurrection—then why did Jesus command them to wait in Jerusalem so they would receive power to be witnesses when the Holy Spirit had come upon them? In Acts chapter one, Jesus Himself referred to that experience as being baptized with the Holy Spirit."

"Reverend Morgan, I've been taught so many things. I've been taught that the gifts of the Spirit passed away when the last apostle died. I've been taught that speaking in other tongues, or 'languages,' was only available to the early church for the purpose of spreading the gospel. I've even heard some teachers say that speaking in other tongues is inspired by the devil."

"Joshua, do you really think I'm being used by the devil?"

"Of course not," I replied quickly.

"I'm going to give you the biblical facts, and then you're going to have to decide for yourself. Here's the truth, Joshua. Jesus called the baptism of the Holy Spirit 'the promise of the Father.' On the Day of Pentecost, the Lord said through Peter that the promise of the Holy Spirit was to them, their children, and to all those afar off—as many as the Lord would call. Joshua, that includes us. Several times in the book of Acts we see people—who were not part of the upper room meeting on Pentecost—receive the Holy Spirit and speak with other tongues. The apostle Paul told the church at Corinth not to forbid anyone to speak in tongues and that we should desire the spiritual gifts. He even said that he spoke in tongues more than all of them. Paul hadn't been in the upper room on the Day of Pentecost. Was he being used by the devil?"

"Certainly not," I replied.

"And," Reverend Morgan continued, "he never mentions tongues being used for spreading the gospel through speaking in other people's languages. Furthermore, Paul was the same apostle who told us to imitate him as he followed Christ. He also explained that when we see Jesus face-to-face, we will not see through a glass dimly anymore, and then the gifts of the Spirit will not be necessary. But until then we need the infilling and power of the Holy Spirit.

"Joshua, you've believed the lie that speaking in other tongues was only given for spreading the gospel in the early church, or that it passed away when the last apostle died. If those things are true, then answer these questions: Who was the last apostle? Are there still apostles today? If the ministry of the apostle has passed away, what about the pastor, teacher, prophet, and evangelist? What about all those who spoke in tongues who weren't apostles? And think about this: Jesus' mother and His brothers were in the upper room on the Day of Pentecost. That means they spoke in tongues too."

"But what about on the Day of Pentecost—didn't those from other countries hear them speaking their own languages?"

"Good question, Joshua. According to Scripture, on the Day of Pentecost there were about one hundred and twenty in the upper room, yet there were less than twenty nations or regions mentioned in Acts chapter two. That would be less than twenty foreign languages. Were all one hundred and twenty only speaking those twenty or so foreign languages? Obviously out of the one hundred and twenty, those from other countries heard some of them magnifying God in their own language. But it also seems logical that many more heavenly languages were spoken.

"Despite all that speculation, what's even more revealing is when Peter stood up to preach the gospel on the Day of Pentecost, he spoke in his own voice, in the known common language, to a crowd of people who were from many different countries. The crowd was made up of devout Jews, and we understand that they had a common language. It wasn't necessary to speak in tongues to spread the gospel. Not to mention that there are no scriptures instructing us to use speaking in tongues to spread the gospel. That's just an excuse people use to say that speaking in tongues is not for today.

"Paul explained that tongues are a sign to unbelievers—which it certainly was at Pentecost—and he also explained that when we speak in tongues, we speak to

God. On the Day of Pentecost what does it say they heard? They heard them speaking the wonderful works of God. Joshua, regardless of what you've been taught, the baptism of the Holy Spirit is important in our lives today. When we speak in tongues, we not only speak to God, we also build ourselves up in our most holy faith. We are vessels the Lord can use in the gifts of His Spirit as He wills."

"I just don't know, Reverend Morgan. It seems to go against so many things I've been taught. It confuses me because I know that you and your family are not being used by the devil. Jesus told us that we would know people by their fruit—their words and actions. You, Mrs. Morgan, and Elisabeth are probably the godliest people I know."

Reverend Morgan smiled as he said, "I appreciate your kind words about my family. I also understand what you're saying, and I see your dilemma. But son, you have to know for yourself. It's like going into battle. People can tell you what it's like, but until you've experienced it for yourself, you really have no idea. The truly important thing is this: You can't accept this just because we say it's real. Joshua, if you respect me as you say—and I believe you do—I want you to do two things for me."

"Sure, Reverend Morgan. Anything…what is it?"

"First, I want you to write down these scriptures…" He began to flip the pages of his Bible. "…and then study them hard. When you study them, I want you forget all of man's doctrine, and allow the truth of the Word of God to speak for itself."

"Yes sir, I'm ready to write," I said, pen in hand.

"Study Jesus' words in John 7:37-39, 14:15-31, 16:7-15, and Acts 1:4-8. Then carefully read the account of the outpouring of the Holy Spirit on the Day of Pentecost in Acts chapter two—the entire chapter. Next read the accounts of believers in the early church receiving the baptism of the Holy Spirit in Acts 8:14-17, 10:44-48, and 19:1-6. Finally, read Paul's instructions to the church concerning the spiritual gifts in First Corinthians chapters 12-14. Don't just read the chapter concerning love and say, 'see all the gifts have passed away.' That argument doesn't make sense in context of the three chapters together. I believe it will become obvious to you that the Lord encourages us to desire and to be used in the gifts, but love becomes the balance."

"I've written them down, and I'll study them diligently."

"Good. I want you to promise me you will do one more thing."

"Yes, sir…anything," I said eagerly.

"One month from now we will begin two weeks of revival meetings. I want you to promise me you will attend one of those meetings."

I was excited to be challenged in my biblical studies. I hadn't received this type of challenge since attending Yale. But to actually place myself in a position to experience what I was studying—that made me nervous.

"Joshua, what I'm about to say is very important."

"Yes sir, I'm listening."

"Son, you cannot choose to accept this teaching based upon my words or based upon your love and hopes for a future with my daughter. Those would be the wrong motives, and would only serve to cause you grief. I'm not challenging you to build your faith in this area of belief, or to experience the Holy Spirit's infilling to please me or to make everything right between you and Elisabeth. All of this is for your own spiritual growth whether or not you ever become my son-in-law. Furthermore, you have to understand that I will love you as a Christian brother regardless of the outcome of our discussions."

"I understand, and thank you, Reverend Morgan. I promise I'll come to one of the revival meetings."

"Good! I've got to be going." He stood and gave me a hug. "I'll see you next month."

As he rode off, I knew I was about to be challenged in my spiritual life like never before. It was exciting and frightening at the same time. I immediately began studying the scriptures, determined that before I went to the revival meeting, I would have a good knowledge of what the Scriptures said about the baptism of the Holy Spirit and the spiritual gifts. I was about to discover the truth of Reverend Morgan's words. Reading about it is one thing, but experiencing it was unlike anything I had ever encountered.

Beauty for Ashes

$\mathcal{I}$t was late spring, 1864, time to keep the promise I made to Reverend Morgan. The two-week revival meeting was about to begin at the Free Methodist Church in Topeka. Assuming it would be a long evening, I planned on staying overnight in a hotel. I started out early in the morning so I could get settled in my room before the evening meeting began.

My enthusiasm for this trip shifted back and forth like the wind on a stormy day. I couldn't say I had absolutely no desire to attend the revival, but I looked forward to getting out of town for a day or two. And then there was the thought of seeing Elisabeth again, which made me nervous. At the same time it had been almost three months since we talked, and I wanted to see her again. On top of all that, I couldn't get the possibility of a move of the Holy Spirit out of my mind. That made me even more nervous.

I had given careful attention to the scriptures Reverend Morgan had given me. I was more open to speaking in tongues than I had ever been, yet I was still struggling with that part of me that said, "Lord, prove it to me." I prayed that prayer so many times I felt conviction rise up in my heart, and then I repented for demanding proof.

As I rode to Topeka I tried to shake off my nervousness by recalling a conversation Elisabeth and I had on the train. She told me about the background of the Free Methodist Church which I found very fascinating. I remember her telling me that Free Methodism was founded in 1860 by a group led by B.T. Roberts. Roberts had been cast off by the Methodist Episcopal Church for criticizing a gross lack of spirituality in their hierarchy. The group chose the name "Free Methodist" because they believed it was improper to charge for better seats in pews closer to the pulpit. They also opposed slavery, which made it a perfect fit for Kansas. Reverend Morgan started the Free Methodist Church in Topeka shortly after the founding of the denomination. According to Elisabeth, it wasn't long after they began when it took off like wildfire. I wondered if the "baptism of fire" is what sparked the wildfire. When that thought entered my mind, I became nervous again.

"It's good to see you again, sir," I said as I shook Reverend Morgan's hand.

"I'm glad you could make it, Joshua. Since you're here, I wonder if I could impose upon you."

"What can I do for you, sir?"

"Come and pray with us before the service begins. We'll meet in a room just to the rear of the choir pews. I'd like to introduce you to my elders. Meet us back there in five minutes." He then hurried off to take care of pre-service arrangements. My nervousness increased, and rightfully so. I had no idea what I was about to encounter.

The Topeka Free Methodist Church had just completed a new building which wasn't too gaudy or too extravagant. To be honest, I thought it was rather plain. There was no stained glass, no extravagant fixtures, and no fancy chairs and pews. Obviously, they had put their money into constructing a practical and functional structure rather than fixating on ornamental luxuries. There was an abundance of pews, however. My guess was that it seated around three hundred. It was a wise decision because the church was filling up quickly.

Unlike the Presbyterian Church, the pulpit was on the same level as the choir. That appealed to me greatly. I never liked appearing as though I was high and mighty. The church fit Reverend Morgan's personality—common, but friendly. He was the same around his parishioners as he was with me—possessing the appearance and speech of a wise man, while at the same time being someone who was easy to relate to.

"Joshua! Over here!" Elisabeth waved to me from a pew down front.

"Mrs. Morgan, Elisabeth, it's good to see you again."

Mrs. Morgan gave me a warm smile. "I'm so glad you could make it, Joshua."

I was uneasy seeing Elisabeth, and I felt as though I needed to make an attempt to clear the air. "Elisabeth, about the last time we talked—"

Elisabeth interrupted. "Joshua, it's okay. I've given it to the Lord. I trust Him."

She seemed genuinely glad to see me. That was quite a relief considering our last conversation. I'm sure her thoughts and feelings hadn't changed but, like her mother, she was always gracious and kind. She pointed to a front row pew and said, "Joshua, please sit here with us."

"Thank you. I'd love to sit here with you. But first, your father asked me to pray with him and the elders. I'll be back when the service begins."

I had a feeling that sooner or later in this meeting I would come face-to-face with the gifts of the Holy Spirit. Part of me felt as though I was walking into a trap—a spiritual trap. On the other hand, I knew that Elisabeth's father would never ask me to participate in anything he felt was detrimental or unscriptural. As a result of our discussions, the study of Scripture, and much prayer I was teetering on the brink of a decision in my heart to receive the baptism of the Holy Spirit. I just didn't desire to be forced over the edge.

As I entered the small room at the rear of the platform, Reverend Morgan introduced me to his elders. He then began to address the group, speaking with wisdom and authority.

"Men, we have witnessed the Lord doing some amazing things in our midst. It is our responsibility—our duty—to enter these services with a pure heart. Our only motives should be to do the will of God, and for Him to be glorified. We want to continue to experience moves of the Holy Spirit, but we also desire that all things are done decently and in order. That's where you come in. I'm counting on you to quench anything that is purely flesh and to encourage all things that are Spirit-led. The Scriptures are clear that no flesh should glory in His presence. Men, we need wisdom. We need the guidance of the Holy Spirit. Let's join hands and let's take a few moments to pray in the Spirit."

There it was! All the men in the room were speaking in tongues except me. I stood silent with my head bowed and my eyes closed. All the scriptures I had studied raced through my mind. Where was the interpretation? If anyone speaks in tongues, there needs to be an interpretation—or was this what Jude referred to as "praying in the Holy Spirit"? I couldn't wait until they stopped. A few minutes seemed like an hour. After the tongue-talking died down, Reverend Morgan began to pray with great fervency for the service. The other men were very vocal in their agreement.

Even though their circle of prayer was different than what I was used to, I could honestly say that nothing appeared to be fanatical or out of order. Reverend Morgan and his elders struck me as being very genuine, certainly not demon possessed. It was obvious to me that these men loved the Lord. They were passionate, but didn't act overly emotional. According to Jesus, if the fruit is good, then the heart must also be good. Their good fruit was even more evident as they introduced themselves to me, shook my hand, and welcomed me with great enthusiasm. I pondered this as the service began.

To me the service seemed rather informal and without structure. After the recitation of the Apostle's Creed, we sang several hymns without a break for Scripture reading or prayer. Reverend Morgan stood in front of his chair on the platform as someone else led the singing. I was familiar with most of the hymns, and the sound of so many people's voices was inspiring and uplifting. The last hymn was fairly new, and was entitled *Savior, Sprinkle Many Nations*. We concluded with the fifth and sixth stanzas:

> Savior, lo! The isles are waiting,
> Stretched the hand and strained the sight,
> For Thy Spirit, new creating,
> Love's pure flame, and wisdom's light.
> Give the word, and of the preacher
> Speed the foot and touch the tongue,
> Till on earth by every creature
> Glory to the Lamb be sung!

As we began the last stanza I looked to my right, and at first glance I didn't see Elisabeth. Then I realized she was kneeling with her hands lifted in the air. Seeing this made me want to weep. She didn't care what people thought of her relationship with God. She desired as much of the Lord as she could grab a hold of. How could I not love a woman such as this? At the same time I knew she was pressing into a place I had not been. She was experiencing the throne of God as I had only longed in my heart to experience. That's what made me want to weep.

As the singing ceased, Reverend Morgan stepped up to the pulpit and began to pray:

"Lord, this is all we desire—Your glory to be seen among the nations. Please, Lord, let it begin with this nation. Father, touch our land that is so deeply divided. Give wisdom to those who seek Your face, and humble those who fight against Your cause. Touch Your church, Lord Jesus. Bind our wounds and heal the brokenhearted. Give strength to all in battle who carry Your name, and empower us by Your Spirit to do Your will. We ask this in the name of Your only Son Jesus, amen."

My opinion of the spiritual gifts notwithstanding, I had to acknowledge a powerful presence of the Holy Spirit. I never had such an encounter with God's Spirit in all my years as a Christian. Something inside of me was hoping for—and even yearning for—a supernatural experience with the Lord. That was certainly not my usual desire or expectation. I could see this was not fanaticism; it was a love for God and a love for His presence.

As Reverend Morgan began to preach, he asked the congregation to turn in their Bibles to John chapter fourteen. Behind me I heard a sea of pages turning. At that moment, I felt like I was in a foreign land. At Old School Presbyterian Church we kept our congregational Bible on a stand at the front of the church for Scripture reading. Members of my church left their Bibles at home in their parlors. As Reverend Morgan paused while we found the passage, I wondered how many of my parishioners actually read their Bibles, or could even find John chapter fourteen.

My eyes were fixed on Reverend Morgan as he preached a powerful message out of the Gospel of John about doing the works that Jesus did. He spoke as plainly and boldly in the pulpit as he did in my parlor. What faith was being built in my heart! I had never considered that, as a believer, I could do the works that Jesus did, and greater works because He went to the Father. And what happened when He went to the Father? He sent the Holy Spirit to empower us to do those works. All of the scriptures I had studied suddenly came together as Reverend Morgan spoke.

At the end of his message he closed his Bible, and it seemed as though he was talking to himself. Later I asked him what he was doing and he explained that when he senses the Holy Spirit's desire to move in a service, he takes a few moments and prays in tongues under his breath. He said he wants to be full of the Holy Spirit and wisdom—to be led by the Spirit in order to accomplish everything the Lord desires.

After a minute or two, he lifted his head, opened his eyes, and said, "There are several here tonight who have been struggling with many things. There are some who have broken hearts—the Lord is going to heal your broken hearts by the anointing and power of His Spirit. There is someone who is struggling with a spiritual issue…"

As much as I admired Reverend Morgan, I felt like standing up and saying, "Now wait a minute…you already knew that!" He knew I was struggling with the baptism of the Holy Spirit. I thought, "Surely he can't be doing this! He's trying to manipulate me!" It's incredible how quickly pride will raise its ugly head. Just when I was about to stop listening to anything else Reverend Morgan had to say, the Lord got my attention as only He can do.

Reverend Morgan continued, "You have said to the Lord, 'Forgive me for being full of pride because I do desire more of you. Forgive me, Lord, for saying that the Holy Spirit baptism will have to be proven to me, otherwise I will not accept it.'"

I caught my breath! Those were the exact words I prayed that morning! No one could have known those words except the Lord. The question of Reverend Morgan's integrity vanished. There was also no more doubt in my mind that the spiritual gifts were still operating amongst believers. The only question which remained was, would my shaky legs be able to carry me as Reverend Morgan invited all those to the front of the church whom the Lord had spoken to?

When I opened my eyes, one of Reverend Morgan's elders had his hand extended, and he helped me to the front pew where I sat down. I looked around and saw there were only a few people left in the church. Elisabeth and her mother were smiling at me. I had gone to the altar and asked the Lord to baptize me with His Holy Spirit. As Reverend Morgan prayed with me, I was overwhelmed by God's powerful presence as I received His Holy Spirit and spoke in other tongues.

"How do you feel, son?" Reverend Morgan asked as he sat down next to me.

"I feel wonderful! God's presence was powerful!" A little curious about what had transpired, I asked, "Is that how it always happens?"

"Joshua, I always endeavor to pray with folks according to scripture. As you recall, when you came forward we lifted our hands in worship and thanksgiving, and you said, 'Father, baptize me with Your Holy Spirit.' The moment I laid my hand on your head and said, 'In the name of Jesus,' you toppled over like a wagon overloaded with bricks. Sometimes God's powerful presence is more than our bodies can handle. Yet, it is important to remember we always receive God's promises by faith, whether we feel anything or not. You studied the scriptures, and faith was built in your heart to receive."

Reverend Morgan was right. Furthermore, the Lord had accomplished a deeper work in my life. In one moment the Lord dealt with my pride about looking foolish.

When I left that night, my heart's desire was to attend every meeting I could for the next two weeks. I expressed my desire to Reverend Morgan on the way out, but I also confided in him that I couldn't afford to pay for two weeks in a hotel. Reverend Morgan motioned to the elder who helped me up off the floor.

"Hey Johnnie, come here a moment."

With the exception of Johnnie Riggs, all of Reverend Morgan's elders were older gentlemen. Johnnie was a stout young man, probably my age. He walked over to where we were standing and asked, "What do you need, Reverend Morgan?"

"Johnnie, Reverend Cole here wants to attend all the services, except Sundays of course. Two weeks in a hotel can be rather expensive. I was thinking since you're a widower that you might enjoy some company."

"Yes sir! Reverend Cole, my house is your house!" Johnnie shook my hand.

With the exception of Sunday mornings, I attended every revival service. Johnnie and I had a wonderful time in the Lord. He had lost his wife and baby two years earlier as she was giving birth. We shared testimonies with each other of how the Lord brought us through difficult times, encouraged each other, and prayed for each other. Another lifelong friendship had begun.

The revival services were outstanding. I learned more about the Word of God and His powerful presence than in all of my years of schooling and ministry. I couldn't get enough! There was a fire inside of me that couldn't be quenched. The fire began to spread as I took Wes Varner to one of the meetings. After that meeting, he told me that for several months he had been seeking more of the Lord through prayer and study, that there always seemed to be something missing—something else he needed. After attending a couple more meetings he realized what it was. At the end of the third meeting, he received the baptism of the Holy Spirit. Now Wes was also on fire for God!

Generally speaking, I wasn't an emotional person. But as Wes was baptized in the Holy Spirit, I began to cry right in front of Elisabeth and her mother. A thought hit me as Wes went down front that triggered an emotional response. I just knew if my parents were alive, they would have responded right along with Wes. I also knew my parents would have fallen in love with the Morgans. The Lord was doing such a great work that I wouldn't allow sorrow to fill my heart. Instead, I thanked Him I could share this experience with Wes.

The difference in my life was hard to describe. The Bible was new and exciting to me again. The words seemed to jump off the page. I couldn't devour scriptures quickly enough. I was, however, still timid about speaking in tongues.

I hadn't spoken in tongues since the night I received the Holy Spirit. On several occasions I thought, "Just let it come out of your mouth." I kept expecting God to take control of my mouth and make me say the words. But then I remembered that Reverend Morgan told me once that the Lord wouldn't make me pray. It was then I realized God wouldn't make me speak in other tongues any more than He would make me pray in English. He had given me control over my mouth, and I would have to submit myself to the promptings of His Spirit.

One day I began to speak the words I heard coming up inside of me. I was near the barn in the rear of the house, and I looked around to make sure no one else was there. I spoke them again. The thought came to me, "That's silly—it's foolishness." Yet I realized Reverend Morgan and all his elders speak it out with such confidence—to them it's not foolishness. Later Reverend Morgan explained to me how a language is something a person grows and develops in, just like a child doesn't speak as well as an adult. That illustration helped tremendously, and I continued to develop and grow in the Holy Spirit.

After the last evening of revival, the Morgans invited Johnnie, Wes, and me to their house for a bite to eat. After two weeks of powerful meetings, and after receiving the baptism of the Holy Spirit, I was smiling from ear to ear. I couldn't help it. I had a joy and contentment in my life I had never experienced. I cast the care of courtship and marriage on the Lord, and I told Him in my prayer time that I was satisfied with Him—He was all I needed. I was delighting myself in the Lord, and He was about to give me the desire of my heart.

As we visited together we talked about how wonderful the Lord had been during the last two weeks. Elisabeth and her mother commented several times on the remarkable change they could see in my life. I just blushed and changed the subject. I knew why, and I was so thankful. I had such a peace in my heart as the evening drew to a close.

"We need to be going," I finally said as Wes and I stood to our feet. "We've had a wonderful evening, but it's getting late. I want to thank all of you for being so patient with me. I feel foolish for ever doubting, but I am so thankful that you didn't give up on me. I can't tell you how much these past two weeks have changed my life."

Reverend Morgan shook my hand and said, "Joshua, before you leave I want you to know that Gloria and I think you're an exceptional young man. Since that first night you were baptized in the Holy Spirit, I knew you weren't the same person. The Lord began doing a deeper work in your life. I can see it in your eyes and in your countenance. We know you and Elisabeth have discussed courtship. We don't want either of you to feel pressured, but if you are still considering it, we want you to know we heartily approve."

I smiled at Elisabeth and she smiled back at me. I saw again the glimmer in her eyes that I longed to see. Courting Elisabeth was not possible without her father's permission. I had given the entire proposition over to the Lord and, in return, He opened the door right in front of me. The time was right and I didn't hesitate to step on through.

With her parents, Wes, and Johnnie as witnesses, I took Elisabeth's hand and asked, "Elisabeth Morgan, may I have the honor of officially courting you?"

"Yes, you may."

When she said yes, I felt like jumping for joy. I had a smile as big as the whole state of Kansas and I was choking back tears at the same time. Wes and Johnnie were thrilled, and I was glad they were able to share the moment with us.

I looked at Elisabeth's parents and said very nervously, "Mr. and Mrs. Morgan, I'm confident we will have a courtship and a marriage someday that is overflowing with the grace and power of God. Thank you for your confidence in me, and I give you my word that I will never disgrace your daughter or your family in any way."

"I know you won't, and I'm proud of you, son." Reverend Morgan gave me a hug and patted me on the back. "We need to pray before you leave."

We all joined hands as Elisabeth's father and mother prayed for the two of us. They prayed for our safety, our purity, and our honor before the Lord.

As I left the Morgan home, Elisabeth smiled and said, "I'll see you soon, Joshua."

Seeing her smile, hearing her say my name, was almost more than I could handle. I was on top of the world. As we rode into the night, all of the wonderful moments of the last two weeks ran through my mind. Wes and I talked about the Lord and the great work He was doing in our lives. Wes couldn't wait to get home and tell his family the good news about my courtship. The three hour ride to Lawrence seemed more like ten minutes.

When I rode up to the house, the Lord gave me a glimpse of my future. Even though it was nighttime, the nightmare was gone. I saw Elisabeth on the porch laughing. I saw children playing in the front yard, and I saw myself sitting on the bench in the lane reading to a little one. I could almost smell cooking coming from the house. The Lord had given me beauty for ashes, the oil of gladness for mourning, and the garment of praise for the spirit of heaviness. And I was eternally grateful.

The Two Shall Become One

While the tragedy of losing my family happened less than one year earlier, and their memory would always be in my heart, I knew the Lord had miraculously delivered me from bondage and brought me into the land of promise. Sadly many families were still tending to the deep wounds of their loss. This bothered me, and at times made me feel guilty, that the peace I felt in my soul was still illusive to so many, and possibly even disingenuous to some. I wasn't deluded, however. If I wasn't cautious, I would find grief trying to sneak up on me. I discovered that that emotion is like a masked bandit, who with stunning craftiness steals without warning. I remained alert, and full of the Holy Spirit.

Without a doubt the Lord deserves all the credit for rescuing me from the pit of anger and depression, and for healing what appeared to be an incurable broken heart. At the same time, a starving man must acknowledge those who hand him a morsel, and give tribute to those who supply water in a dry and weary land. As I reflected on how mightily the Lord used the Morgan family—as Samaritans who bound the wounds of a "certain man who fell among thieves"—I also saw how a terrible tragedy became the occasion through which Elisabeth and I drew close to each other in ways which otherwise would not have been possible.

There were some folks who considered the announcement of courtship to be somewhat abrupt. However, to us it was the next obvious step in a relationship that had grown strong in the most difficult times. Long before courtship Elisabeth had witnessed me at my worst. She listened as I told her my deepest feelings and harshest thoughts, and she prayed for me as the Lord reached out His hand to pull me from the fire. As I considered all of this, I was caught up in the wonder of how the Lord knit our hearts together in the midst of adversity. I was also strengthened in my deep love and commitment to Elisabeth, the woman who loved me and desired to be my wife despite having seen me at my lowest.

Elisabeth and I already felt like we knew each other well, yet we also understood we had much more to learn. And even though we were both in our mid-twenties, we highly regarded the tradition and virtue of courtship. For us it was not just a frivolous way to become better acquainted with our future spouse. It was about honoring her mother and father, showing proper respect for one another, and remaining pure before marriage by practicing biblical principles while seeking accountability and wise counsel.

Elisabeth and I spent as much time together as possible. Her parents were wonderful chaperones and counselors. Though we enjoyed the time we spent with each other, we both agreed that the best part of our courtship was the time we spent with her parents. Within our courtship we showed unreserved respect for her family's reputation. In return, her parents were very gracious and wise about overseeing our courtship while allowing us to grow close to one another.

We were overjoyed to be getting married, but also nervous. Since my parents were gone, I needed all the insight about marriage I could get. And since Elisabeth was an only child, we had her parent's full attention. Reverend and Mrs. Morgan had been married thirty-two years, and they were more than willing to share their wisdom with us.

Throughout our courtship I visited the Morgans at least once a week. During one such visit Reverend Morgan counseled us saying, "Listen kids, you'll have arguments. The younger your marriage is, the more important they seem to be. The longer you're married, the more you realize it's not about winning the argument— it's about honoring the Lord in all you do. The longer Gloria and I are married, the less selfish each of us becomes. And the less we desire to argue. Now, when children come along—"

"Whoa, Dad," Elisabeth interrupted with a smile on her face, "A wise father once said, 'Let's take it one thing at a time.'"

Mrs. Morgan rescued her blushing daughter as she asked, "You've been courting now for several months. Have you thought about a wedding date?"

I was glad Mrs. Morgan had prodded us a little. We had talked about a date, but hadn't discussed it with her parents.

"We thought the middle of October would be nice. The trees will be turning, and we can get settled in the house before winter," Elisabeth replied.

"That's wonderful," her father said enthusiastically. "Our church is certainly open to you, son."

"Thank you, sir. I hope this doesn't sound selfish, but I was wondering if we could have the wedding at the Old School Presbyterian Church in Lawrence. That way, Elisabeth and I wouldn't have far to travel after the wedding."

"That makes good sense. Who do you have in mind to perform the ceremony?"

Without hesitation I replied, "We were hoping you would, sir."

"I was hoping you would ask me," Reverend Morgan said, smiling.

As the months passed, we spent more and more time with Elisabeth's parents. They continued to teach us biblical principles concerning marriage and shared many stories from their own experiences. Their wisdom was appreciated and well-received at the time, but as the years went by it proved to be even more invaluable. We also spent a lot of time in prayer together.

Two weeks before the wedding, the planning and busyness accelerated like a locomotive speeding down a hill. Mrs. Morgan made Elisabeth a beautiful dress and I shopped for a new suit in Lawrence. Elisabeth and her mother also supplied me with a long list of "wedding chores." It seemed that everyday I was running errands, or cleaning and polishing things in the church and at home. I certainly didn't mind. I looked forward to the day when Elisabeth and I would be joined together as one, and I wanted everything to be perfect for my bride.

"Reverend Cole!"

I had just come out of a store on Massachusetts Street and turned to see who was yelling for me. It was Colonel Eldridge.

"Colonel, it's good to see you," I said as I shook his hand. "You've just about completed your hotel. It looks fantastic!"

"Reverend, I meant to speak to you after church on Sunday, but I couldn't catch you before you rode off."

"I'm sorry, Colonel. I've been spending a lot of time with Elisabeth and her family, and I was anxious to get to Topeka."

"That's what I want to talk about."

Oh no. Did he think I was neglecting the church? Was he concerned about my safety riding back and forth from Topeka? It's amazing how a minister can begin to think the worst right off, before he even knows what something is all about. As soon as these thoughts entered my mind, the Lord rebuked me in my heart and said, "Be still and listen."

"Two things, Reverend. First, I want to tell you that I've noticed a change in your preaching. It has been very inspiring. I'm not sure what's happened to you, but keep it up! A lot of people have commented."

"Thank you very much!" I was so relieved.

"The second thing is, my brother and I and our families want to bless you and your bride. We would like your permission to have a get-together after the wedding for you and all who attend the ceremony in our new ballroom at the hotel. We'll supply all the food, cake, and we'll even have a piano player who plays that really fancy kind of music. What do you think?"

"What do I think?" I said with excitement, "My goodness! I don't know what to say except thank you very much! I can't wait to tell Elisabeth!"

"Great! It's all set. I remember you announced the date, but get back with me real soon to confirm the time, and we'll take care of the rest." The colonel hurried off. He was a man of action. He made a plan, and then he set it in motion.

Once again, the Lord blessed us right out of the blue. We were delighting ourselves in the Lord, and He was supplying everything we needed—above and beyond what I could've imagined. I certainly didn't doubt the colonel's sincerity, or generosity, but I did wonder why he became so personally involved. His excitement seemed to have been stirred by something. I was curious what it was.

⌒

"Can I help you?" said the clerk behind the counter.

"I'm Joshua Cole, and I'm looking for Colonel Eldridge. I have some information he asked for."

"Yes sir, I'll go find him for you."

I looked around as I waited at the front desk, amazed at how the hotel looked. It was much more extravagant than the previous building. There was a beautiful polished brass chandelier in the lobby with crystals hanging from it, stained glass on the upper portion of the windows, oak trim everywhere, and luxurious furniture with dark red velvet cushions.

As I glanced over my shoulder I noticed someone leaning on the second floor railing, staring at me. I turned around slowly so I could get a better look. At first glance I didn't recognize the stranger who was dressed in a long dark coat. Then it struck me—I couldn't believe my eyes!

"Harry!"

As I shouted, he ran down the stairs to meet me.

"Where did you…How did you…When did you get in town!"

"I have a personal invitation to my best friend's wedding," Harry said as he gave me a playful shove (which still hurt a little).

"How did you know about it? I've thought of you so many times, and I would've invited you, but I didn't know where to find you!"

"Colonel Eldridge put in an order for me to be transferred and attached to the troops here in Lawrence. He said he ran into your bride and her family, and she asked him if he might be able to locate me and make the arrangements."

That explained how the colonel got so closely involved. Just then the colonel walked into the lobby. He wore a satisfied look on his face and shook his head in approval.

"I'm glad you two found each other," he said as he walked over and slapped both of us on our backs.

"Sir, I can't thank you enough for everything you've done. I just can't believe it!"

"It's my pleasure, Reverend. Tell me, what time is the wedding, and what time should we expect the guests?"

"The wedding will be one week from today—Saturday, October 15th, at 11:00 a.m. And with your permission, we'll invite everyone to the hotel afterward. You should probably expect folks around noon or a little after. That way, if you don't mind, we'll have plenty of time to eat and visit before sunset."

"Excellent! We'll have everything ready." The colonel waved good-bye and dashed off again.

Everything was coming along perfectly. I took Harry back to the house and told him all about my experiences the last two years. He told me stories of the war and the work God had done in his life.

"Harry, I'm so glad the Lord has protected you during this war."

"So am I, Josh!" Harry said as he laughed. "It's been close a few times, and you know the Lord even supernaturally directed me out of deadly situations."

Harry was the only one who called me Josh. As soon as he said my name, it took me back to our college days. Yet because of what we had both been through, college seemed like an entirely different lifetime.

"I can't tell you how excited I am that you're baptized in the Holy Spirit. I saw the difference in you right away," Harry said with a look of contentment on his face.

"I *feel* different, Harry. It's hard to explain to folks how it strengthens your walk with the Lord. But you already know that. I wish I'd listened to you years ago."

"That doesn't matter now. Prayers have been answered, and I am so thankful." Then he reached over and laid his hand on mine. "About your parents, I felt so sad when I heard the news. I knew about the massacre, but I didn't know you had lost your entire family until the colonel told me. I wished I would've known. I would've asked to be transferred here a long time ago."

"Harry, you can't transfer out of a war just because of the hardships here."

"I would've for you, Josh."

I believed him. What a friend!

"I'm sure the colonel also told you that Jordan is missing. We never found him."

"He did tell me, Josh, but don't give up hope. While I'm here I want to help look for him. I'm going to write some officers I know in Missouri and make them aware of the situation. We'll put the word out like never before and see what turns up."

"Thanks, Harry, and don't worry—I won't give up hope. Speaking of hope, do you think you'll find someone and get married after the war?"

"Oh sure," Harry said confidently, "I've already prayed about it."

"I could've figured that."

I smiled every time I thought of the unsuspecting woman somewhere that Harry was praying and believing God for. She would have to be someone awfully special for her path to cross with my best friend.

"I need to ask you something, Harry. Will you stand up with me?"

He didn't answer right away—only swallowed hard as he choked back tears.

"A regiment of Confederates couldn't keep me from it. I would be honored."

"Fantastic! I have one more favor to ask."

"Anything you want, Josh, just say it."

"The Morgans are coming into town the day before the wedding. We're going to unload Elisabeth's things here on Friday morning. We could sure use your muscles."

"Are you kidding? I'll be here. I could use the exercise."

On the morning of October 14th, the Morgans rolled down the lane—their wagon full. Colonel Eldridge had given them adjoining rooms at the hotel so they could stay over that night. This way, they wouldn't have to bring all of Elisabeth's belongings the day of the wedding, while also trying to prepare for the wedding itself. As Reverend Morgan climbed down off the wagon and gave me a hug, he looked over at Harry.

"You must be Harry. We've heard a lot about you." Reverend Morgan reached out to shake my friend's hand.

Harry and Reverend Morgan were two peas in a pod—both were very outgoing and bold in their faith. Even though they were meeting for the first time, a hand-shake was not sufficient for two men such as this. Harry threw his arms around Reverend Morgan and gave him a big bear hug. Reverend Morgan laughed and hugged him back. Next, Harry greeted Mrs. Morgan, then walked over to Elisabeth and took her hand.

"It's nice to finally meet you," he told her. "I'm telling you, Josh hasn't stopped talking about you. Elisabeth, I believe the Lord will bless your marriage beyond what you could ever imagine. And if there's anything I can ever do for you two, you just say the word."

Elisabeth smiled at me, then looked back at Harry and said, "Thank you so much. You've been such a blessing in Joshua's life, and I hope you're able to stay in Lawrence for awhile so we can spend some time together."

Reverend Morgan seemed unusually quiet, almost melancholy, as we stood around the wagon getting ready to unload. As we were about to begin, he looked at me for a minute without saying a word. It looked as though he was getting teary-eyed. Then he reached out and shook my hand, and said, "Let's get her unloaded, son."

After unloading several trunks full of Elisabeth's clothes and personal items, her parents presented us with a magnificent antique cherry china cabinet, decorated with etched glass, as a wedding gift. It had been handed down to Mrs. Morgan by her parents on her wedding day. As we began carefully unloading the cabinet, I caught a glimpse of Elisabeth walking Charlemagne around the corner of the house to the barn. One never guesses what event or moment will cause the realities of life to sink in. For me, it was that moment—those two or three seconds I watched Elisabeth disappear around the corner of the house—that the splendor of what was happening registered in my heart. Everything was set. Everything was ready. Tomorrow my house would be her home.

"I wish we could stay a little longer, Joshua, but we still have a few minor things to take care of at the hotel," Elisabeth told me as I gave her a hand up into the wagon.

I looked up at her and held onto her hand. "The next time I see you, you'll be walking down the aisle. I want you to know that I love you with all my heart, and I've never been happier in all my life."

"I love you too, Joshua. Since I was a little girl I have dreamed of my wedding day and the man I would marry. God has blessed me with the man of my dreams."

Reverend Morgan snapped the reins and Elisabeth's hand slipped out of mine. One more day and our dreams would become reality.

The sun sparkled off the brass on the horse-drawn buggies. I counted fifteen in the field behind the church, eight wagons, and at least ten single horses tied to the posts in front. Between Topeka Free Methodist Church and Old School Presbyterian Church, we had a full house. The church had never been so crowded. The inside was comfortable—thanks to a cool October breeze.

Harry was waiting for me. Even though chaplains were treated as captains, they usually wore a plain black frock coat with one row of nine brass buttons down the front—the same coat Harry was wearing when I met him at the Eldridge House. Today, however, he was dressed in a captain's uniform complete with shiny brass insignia and a polished sword. Reverend Morgan also looked very distinguished in his best suit as he walked over and said, "It's time to begin."

I hadn't seen Elisabeth. Her mother had kept her hidden in a small room off the vestibule. Reverend Morgan led Harry and me down front. As we stood by the altar, he slowly walked down the center aisle to the rear and into the vestibule.

Next, Mrs. Morgan came slowly down the aisle wearing a light blue gown. Elisabeth wanted her mother to stand with her as she got married. She had many friends, but none as dear to her as her mother.

After reaching the altar, Mrs. Morgan stopped and smiled tenderly at me as I took a deep breath and stood wide-eyed staring at the vestibule. I saw Reverend Morgan step out first…and then—there she was.

My heart skipped a beat as the congregation stood to their feet. I took in every step and every movement. Elisabeth was more beautiful than anything I had ever seen. Harry playfully nudged me in the back, and I quickly tapped him on the hand so he would leave me alone. I was determined to savor every second as I watched my bride walk down the aisle.

Her beauty is imprinted in my memory. With her flowing white gown, she looked like the princesses I had seen in magazines. I was taken aback by her lovely blonde hair flowing from underneath her delicate veil through which I could scarcely see her gentle smile and her beautiful eyes. This veiled beauty only added to the anticipation in my heart. I couldn't wait to hold her hand and look into her eyes. She was carrying two roses, one of which she would give to her mother. Symbolically she was saying that she was leaving her mother and father and becoming one with her husband.

They stopped when they reached the altar and her father turned toward the congregation.

"Ladies and gentlemen, thank you for coming and celebrating this day with us. It is with great joy in our hearts that Gloria and I give our daughter this day to Joshua Cole." He lifted Elisabeth's veil and kissed her on the cheek. He then took Elisabeth's hand and placed it in mine. As he stepped up to the podium, I looked into Elisabeth's eyes. My knees became weak, and I didn't hear a word of the message until it was time to say our vows.

"Joshua and Elisabeth, I want to remind both of you that these vows are not only being spoken before these witnesses, but more importantly before God. Joshua Goodwin Cole, do you covenant with Elisabeth, whose hand you hold, to be her husband? To join yourself to her as one flesh? To love her as Christ loved the church? To honor her, protect her, and provide for her, forsaking all others, and cleaving only to her as long as you both shall live?"

"I do." I gazed into Elisabeth's tear-filled eyes and placed a ring on her finger.

"Elisabeth Abigail Morgan, do you covenant with Joshua, whose hand you hold, to be his wife? To join yourself to him as one flesh? To love him and submit to him as Christ commands? To respect him, honor him, and provide a home for him while forsaking all others; cleaving only to him as long as you both shall live?"

Elisabeth replied with two of the most beautiful words I've ever heard, "I do," mouthing the words "I love you" as she placed the ring on my finger. We were both about to cherish a moment we had dreamed of—our first kiss.

"Joshua and Elisabeth, the gift of marriage is granted to us by our Father in heaven. Marriage is a two-part reflection of the unity between the Father, Son, and the Holy Spirit. It is your duty to see to it that no one ever interferes with this precious gift the Lord has granted. And now, by the power vested in me, I pronounce you husband and wife. Joshua, you may kiss your bride."

He didn't have to tell me twice! It was wonderful and certainly worth waiting for!

"Ladies and gentlemen, it is my privilege to introduce to you Mr. and Mrs. Joshua Goodwin Cole." We turned to face the crowd, and then walked down the aisle—together.

Our reception at the Eldridge House was right out of a fairytale. Everyone and everything was magnificent. We spent all afternoon and early evening enjoying the food, the company, and most of all the exhilaration of being Mr. and Mrs. Cole.

As the sun began to sink low in the west, folks started saying good-bye. Many of the guests had to travel back to Topeka, and probably stayed longer than they should have. After everyone left, we spent a good ten minutes thanking the colonel for his overwhelming generosity.

"Father, Mother…as anxious as I am to start my new life, it's so hard to say good-bye," Elisabeth said as she hugged her parents.

"I know, but we're only a few hours away. We'll see each other soon," Reverend Morgan said with tears in his eyes. "But you two need lots of time by yourself. Besides, you know we're always there if you need us."

Once again Elisabeth's mother and father prayed for us before we left to begin our new life together. Afterward we all hugged, and then we knew it was time to go. I helped Elisabeth onto the wagon bench, and then I climbed up next to her, snapped the reins, and began driving the wagon toward home.

It was a cool evening, and we sat close to each other on the wagon bench. With one hand Elisabeth held her rose, and with the other she held my arm. I glanced at her as often as I could, just to make sure this moment was real. I could not begin to describe the profound and powerful love I had in my heart.

With Elisabeth by my side, I reflected on the journey of my life thus far. God had supplied me with a rich family heritage, and a new family that gave me strength and courage. He had also blessed my life by opening up His Word and filling me with His Holy Spirit. The Great Shepherd had led me through the valley of the shadow of death, and was now leading me beside still waters and making me lie down in green pastures.

A brilliant sunset streamed across the sky beyond the tall elm trees as we rode in the wagon down Somerset Lane. After Elisabeth climbed down off the wagon with my help, she walked over to the bench at the end of the lane, paused for a moment, and then placed her rose on the bench.

"What are you thinking about?" I asked softly.

"I was thinking of your parents. I'm so thankful for the life they led, and that they had a son named Joshua."

"Thank you, Elisabeth…I love you."

I took her in my arms. After we kissed, Elisabeth held onto me for a moment as she prayed, "Lord, give us the grace to have a marriage and family that will bring glory and honor to You."

"Amen," I said.

We looked at each other and smiled. We knew in our hearts that there was a sunrise on the horizon of our lives which would prove to be more exciting than anything we had experienced.

We would continue to search for Jordan. Elisabeth and I trusted the Lord for answers concerning his disappearance. And I looked forward to Harry being in Lawrence for a while so we could strengthen each other in our walk with God.

Most of all, I looked forward to building a life and family with Elisabeth. As we walked into our new life together, my heart cried out, "May God truly be exalted in all that we do."

About the Author

Jeff Canfield is a graduate of Rhema Bible Training Center and Logos Christian College, and has served in pastoral ministry since 1999. He is the author of two non-fiction books, *A Call to Honor* and *Life Isn't Rocket Science*, and the co-author of *What Left Behind Left Out—The Truth* (non-fiction).

If you have questions or comments, or would like to contact Jeff, send an e-mail to isiradio@juno.com.

To order additional copies of

Somerset Elm

The Journey Begins

have your credit card ready and call
1 800-917-BOOK (2665)

or e-mail
orders@selahbooks.com

or order online at
www.selahbooks.com

Printed in the United States
92168LV00001B/31-48/A